I AM NOT THERE

GINNY STROUD

6477344

Matador
9 Priory Business Park,
Wistow Road, Kibworth Beauchamp,
Leicestershire. LE8 0RX
Tel: 0116 279 2299
Email: books@troubador.co.uk
Web: www.troubador.co.uk/matador
Twitter: @matadorbooks

ISBN 978 1784625 245

British Library Cataloguing in Publication Data.
A catalogue record for this book is available from the British Library.

Printed and bound by CPI Group (UK) Ltd, Croydon, CR0 4YY
Typeset in 11.5pt Aldine401 BT by Troubador Publishing Ltd, Leicester, UK

Matador is an imprint of Troubador Publishing Ltd

In Memory of my Grandmother

Gertrude Annie Stroud

With the hope that this is not a work of fiction

INTRODUCTION

Alzheimer's – just a word but one which conjures a whole range of emotions and thoughts – none of them positive. But how do we know: we are easily fooled. When you look in a mirror you do not see reality. OK it is not distorted like a hall of mirrors, but the image is false – it is reversed. Maybe it is us who "see through a glass darkly". Maybe it is we "normal" beings who are living in a fog of misunderstanding.

Scientists and cynics may dispute this interpretation, but, like the looking glass their conclusions are limited by the frame of their current knowledge. We cannot yet see beyond those confines.

When we come to the mind, whether human or animal, all their learning and rational thinking has no more creditability than we lesser mortals. Put simply – no one knows.

Without proof any ridicule of supernatural beliefs is worst than "blind faith" because it smacks of a bias which is anything but scientific. It shows a closed viewpoint which belittles what it cannot explain or understand.

So I ask my readers to open your minds, free your imagination, and just ask a question "What if?"

Do not stand at my grave and weep.
I am not there. I do not sleep.
I am a thousand winds that blow.
I am the diamond glints on snow.
I am the sunlight on ripened grain.
I am the gentle autumn rain.
When you awaken in the morning's hush
I am the swift uplifting rush
Of quiet birds in circled flight.
I am the soft stars that shine at night.
Do not stand at my grave and cry;
I am not there. I did not die.

Mary Elizabeth Frye
1932

Chapter One

March 1993

ELIZABETH

I began this diary many years ago, as a child. One of the many practices passed on from my grandmother, along with the original, complete, version of her name Betsy.

She adopted me legally as a ten month old baby and unconsciously set about shaping my character. There were no print or electronic aids to this process: just natural good sense, and plenty of love. The result is a living testimony to the combined strength of nature and nurture. I have inherited the no nonsense, sometimes stubborn, attitude to life which has travelled through many female generations of our family. Yet this is tempered by an instilled sensitivity for other creatures. My earliest memories are pre school lessons on respecting animals, which always included consequences. Any complaint of our pet dog growling was greeted by the gentle question "what were you doing to her?" My grandmother had the judgement of Solomon when dealing with two or four legged complainants.

Empathy, especially when coupled with an imaginative nature, is a mixed blessing. The process of "putting yourself in another's shoes, or paws" can cause as much pain as pleasure.

In this respect, though, I would not choose to be anything other than I am: Elizabeth Ann Lewis.

There is one trait, however, I sincerely hope not to inherit which, in recent years, has become the overriding topic of this journal. How could it not? It is totally invasive and, as yet, incurable. In common with another dreaded terminal disease just its name brings anxiety and alarm: Alzheimer's.

Sometimes, in my darker moods, I consider the future heredity possibilities: even going so far as to estimate the time I have left. A countdown to slow oblivion.

My grandmother's symptoms began at age seventy eight. On that basis I have roughly thirty five years to write this book.

Now that seems like a long time, but time is a fluid and finite element. Like sand in an hourglass, once turned, its progress is relentless. Before you know it, the sand has run out and you are left with nothing, but regrets.

So I had better get on with it! But to go forward I must first travel back – I pick up my diary for 1983 and begin in the month of June.

It should have been a happy, therapeutic, event. I had just passed my driving test. A late bloomer I now held my licence at age thirty three.

It was all the more precious because my first attempt was a frustrating failure.

There were two examiners in our local test centre: I was to learn later that one was a rational human being. Unfortunately on my first outing I was doomed for his colleague: a dour, misogynist "jobs worth", whose main talent was sarcasm.

Such characters, if they cannot be ridiculed, are best forgotten and my brain cells are disintegrating too quickly to waste space on the storage of rubbish.

So to return to what is important. I had booked a week's holiday in a static caravan on the Hampshire coast. It was a small private park, in a lovely peaceful setting, bordering the beautiful New Forest.

BETSY

My grand daughter, Elizabeth – or Beth – never Liz or Lizzy, and I have been together now for half of my life and all of hers.

Her mother, my daughter, Margaret, was only twenty when she had Beth. Too young and too hurt by the desertion of the father to deal with a baby. So in my late forties I found myself a mother for the second time. My husband, George and I, would have chosen a bigger family: not a litter, but at least one more. However the growth of a large fibroid meant the removal of my womb and the end of that hope.

As unplanned as this new infant was, she was never unloved. I come from a generation where "a stiff upper lip" was a reality, not a joke. We learnt through the Victorian example of our parents not to show public emotion. Nowadays this behaviour has been described as "cold," or even unnatural, but to us, children of The Great War, anything else would have been embarrassingly foreign.

This does not mean we felt less physical pain, or emotional distress, we were just taught greater self control. Don't misunderstand me. Sometimes an outpouring of grief is really good for you: a great relief. But the reality is willing ears, even those of close friends, can become rapidly deaf when bent too often.

Then genuine sympathy can turn into pity, and

4

the relationship changes, to no one's good. That we loved each other there was never any doubt, but we chose private affection rather than public drama, and action, rather than words.

When my daughter left to begin a new life and family, Beth was six and I had passed my half century. George, a year younger, just fifty, was beginning to look forward to retirement. Thankfully, perhaps, we never knew those plans would be a waste of time.

I lost my husband eight years later. Lost – what a stupid expression – sounds as if I misplaced him like an umbrella or glasses! That he could be so easily replaced!

It was sudden – he literally dropped dead while digging an elderly neighbour's garden. No good deed goes unpunished. The post mortem said "coronary thrombosis." Our GP explained it as a large blood clot which hit his heart and stopped it immediately. If so it had a large target: George was the best of the best: a real "gentle" man.

With his death our family went from three to two. My daughter was now remarried and looking after her two small children in America: One thing the unexpected loss taught us was the importance of the present.

We, as the old saying goes, "never let the sun go down on our anger" – put more practically: we always kissed each other goodnight.

I suppose if anyone saw us on the street together, they may have felt pity or admiration. They would have been wrong in both. We were lucky: we had each other and there was nothing brave about it – we just carried on.

As the years went by we grew closer: supporting

each other. I was proud of her successes, and let her know it.

Passing her driving test was no different – she was a good little driver and I let everyone else know it.

It was June, our cases were packed, and I was looking forward to our first holiday together in years.

Perhaps once again, luckily, neither of us knew it would also be our last: what happened there would change both our remaining lives.

Chapter Two

June 1983

ELIZABETH

When was the beginning of the end?

It's hard to remember now. In the last few years physical and mental exhaustion have almost obliterated every prior memory. Ironically while my grandmother remembers "the good old days" I can only recall the last nine years.

I have this diary, however, to remind me and now looking through it – I do remember – it began on that holiday.

In the middle of June we loaded our pre-packed suitcases into the old green Marina. I mention the car, but not the cases. I know, though, it would have been cases, not bags. My grandmother's generation used bags for shopping not holidays. Journeys were special events and, as such, deserved the best – including clothes. You went away dressed up to the nines, as if for a wedding, sometimes even including a hat. At the time this seemed not the least bit peculiar.

We set off, in style, around noon: much earlier than the 4pm handover necessitated. But it gave us time for a leisurely drive and lunch.

Even so we were still well ahead of schedule by the time we entered the New Forest. A perfect excuse, as if one were needed, to stop for a real clotted cream tea in one of the many traditional tea rooms advertised along the route.

We arrived at the Hampshire coast a few minutes prior to 4pm and, no doubt, a few pounds heavier.

So that first day went well, and it appears from my memoirs, the first couple of days followed suit.

Those first diary entries are a pure pleasure to read. They are full of an optimism I have almost forgotten. A belief in happiness, so strong, it extended from the present into the future.

In our blissful ignorance we even dared to imagine this might be the first of many such excursions. The phrase about "counting unhatched chickens" comes to mind!

It wasn't until the third night that the shadow first fell over us, and my writing changed.

The first night we went to bed so tired we slept until a sunshine dawn filtered through thin curtains. The drive itself had not been long: just about ninety minutes from the Cotswolds to south coast. But excitement, and feeding breaks, had taken their toll. By the time we unpacked, had our final meal "a last supper" we were ready for our respective beds by 10 pm.

Our accommodation was a six berth caravan, which was compact enough to be cosy, but spacious enough for comfort. I was still at an age where sleep came easily anywhere, so I gave Gran the largest, en suite bedroom.

My journal reminds me we had a lazy Sunday, followed by a peaceful second evening. Apparently we watched television. It would have been a large, pre LCD, monster, which must have taken up a fair area of the living room.

There was nothing written about the next day which gave any warning of subsequent events. Just brief descriptions of places we had visited, and, yes, food we had eaten. Ah, the long forgotten joy of writing about such trivia! To all appearances just a routine holi-day.

That night, having found some board games in a cupboard, we abandoned the tv for an old fashioned and more sociable game of draughts.

I don't mention it, but I know we would then have shared cups of cocoa. It would have been cups because Gran was from an age where mugs were impolite. Then, in those famous words: "and so to bed."

It was not a peaceful night – according to the next day's entry. Something had disturbed me enough to bring me fully awake. Not just a brief partial consciousness, where you turn over and return to sleep. But the kind of awareness which had me fumbling for my bedside travel clock. The green glowing dial told me it was only 2 am – what had awoken me?

It is said the human body and brain are at their lowest ebb between the hours of 2 and 4 am. The time of least resistance, when death is at its peak. No wonder the expression "the darkest hour is before the dawn" is so well known, because it is so true.

Perhaps this affected my reactions, because time seemed to slow down. In such moments of confusion and alarm it is common to find yourself in some bizarre old celluloid movie. One which is suddenly caught and dragging in its sprockets.

What was in fact just a matter of seconds, morphed into minutes, before I roused myself enough to get out of bed. The situation was compounded by the strangeness of my surroundings, and I was still orientating myself as I groped for the door.

I turned its handle and found Gran wandering around in the kitchen, which was immediately outside my bedroom.

No great surprise: middle of the night excursions were a norm at home. This was the result of an ageing urinary system: either requiring a drink or toilet dash. Sometimes both, although, hopefully, not at the same time! So no great surprise – except she was totally in the dark.

I found the nearest switch and threw us both into a florescent glow. It didn't help. The expected exclamation of recognition never came.

My grandmother's eyes blinked in the sudden light, but continued to look confused. Her vision then settled on me, but instead of comforting recognition she kept that puzzled expression of bewilderment.

For the first time I felt a strange desperation which would become so depressingly familiar over the next nine years. What I could not describe then, I realise now, was my introduction to a sense of helpless fear. There was obviously something not quite right: something I did not recognise in that face I knew so well and I loved so much.

When she asked "where am I". It should have been funny, but it wasn't. Something about the vulnerability of a woman whom I had always regarded as my anchor squashed all possibility of humour.

In one moment all established roles were suddenly

reversed and I replied with the gentle patience you should adopt when dealing with a child: "Come on Gran we are on holiday – in the New Forest".

I remember now, I helped her back to her room and bed. I remember I put out the light and stood by the cracked door until her breathing deepened into a low snore. I remember I went back to bed, and that I didn't fall asleep myself until the dangerous "witching" hours had passed – it was 4 am

I slept until 7am, when I pushed back the curtains and daylight eclipsed events of the previous night. But with sunshine there are always shadows, and what was lurking within them could only be ignored for so long. For the moment, though, I could hear activity in the kitchen and something else: singing.

Although the words I wrote so long ago give no clue to my anxiety, yet reading "between the lines" I recall everything as clear as this moment.

I made a decision. When I opened the door and walked into that kitchen I was stepping out onto a stage. For better or worst, for my grandmother or myself, we had been granted a reprieve. A chance to ignore the future possibilities and focus on the present.

I think we both tried: I don't recall either of us mentioning the incident. If we didn't discuss it, then we could pretend it never happened.

What fools we are! Of course it was still there, and by failing to deal with it we let go the chance to share our feelings and fears. As the days and weeks went by those opportunities became less and less possible.

In a way our holiday ended that night. From that

moment we both began retreating into our different worlds – although neither of us acknowledged it. It wasn't that we loved each other less, in fact just the opposite. But we could not share this problem because it was taboo. It was too close to history repeating itself.

My gran had been brought up by her own grandmother and had later watched her mental deterioration. Family circumstances meant that she was eventually committed to a local mental health hospital in the last year of her existence. For existence was all it was, and in those bad old days such establishments carried the stigma word "asylum."

Despite the necessity of this decision I don't think my grandmother ever really forgave herself. I know she had a horror of such places. Not without justification: in those days the general reaction towards mental disease was ignorance and alarm. Society therefore demanded segregation, which sheltered poor living conditions and barbaric remedies.

Although the treatment of psychiatric illness had changed, my grandmother's dread of such institutions had not.

The sad paradox was, while she was the best counsellor I could have had on this subject, I could not ask her. How do you suggest to someone you love that they have a mental disorder?

For the first time in our lives this was something we could not share.

I could not ask for help, and she could not tell me how she felt – if indeed she even knew.

I have heard it said, if you have to consider whether you have Alzheimer's, then you don't.

It comes like a thief in the night: that's certainly how it began with us.

Outwardly we were a grandmother and grand daughter enjoying an early summer break. Inwardly I just wanted to get home: where, I hoped, familiar surroundings would bring back normality. Where there would be no more shadows.

My grandmother and I shared one inborn blessing, or curse. We are both extremely perceptive to people and atmospheres. Believers would call this psychic, others would dismiss it as being overly sensitive. Whichever view you subscribe to, I think it was this "gift" which gave me an insight, and dread for the future. I was afraid and I hated it.

BETSY

When did it all begin?

I remember so well – so clearly: it was that lovely holiday in the New Forest.

The time I began to really understand the reality of life and death.

How can I describe it to you – I can't, anymore than I could tell Beth. It's like trying to explain colour to someone born blind. You know what life was like, you know what its like now: but only you experience the difference. But I am jumping ahead.

I was enjoying the holiday: it was everything I wanted. Beautiful countryside, a comfortable caravan, not like the small one we had booked in North Wales when my husband was alive. We even had an inside loo – thank goodness, my waterworks are not so reliable now!

What made it perfect was sharing all this with Beth. We always fed off each other's pleasure, and I could tell she was so happy. If I have any regrets about my new life, it is because it does not yet include Beth. Over the past few years I have seen the pain and anger it has caused her. I am so sorry for this, but know she will understand soon. Time has no real meaning for me anymore. Odd really considering I drive Beth mad asking to know it every few minutes!

Back to our first lazy Sunday. We rested the car, and ourselves, and after cooked breakfast, went for a walk around the site. It was quiet, apart from church bells coming from a nearby village. The walk didn't take too long: it was a small family run site, but well looked after with flower beds and shrubs.

It suited me down to the ground. I love gardens: all their sights, scents and sounds. The nearest thing to Heaven I can think of – I hope its like that!

We had bought enough groceries with us for breakfasts and Sunday roast. So on the return to the caravan I made a start on the lamb, while Beth acted as my vegetable cook. I didn't mind: cooking was another love. Many years ago, while in service, I took over the job in a small middle class household and found my niche.

We had a late lunch, well late for us – around 2pm. By the time we had washed up and watched a film on the large television it was 6pm, so we skipped tea and had supper. Just a sandwich, but a doorstep one, with cheese and pickle. Washed down with a cup of cocoa.

Monday was another lovely day. June is usually so much nicer than July and August. A mixture of spring and summer, with the best of both flowers.

Once more we filled up with a egg and bacon breakfast. We spent the day driving around the New Forest. Lunchtime we found a small village pub – I even remember its name, Boldre, and what we had: surprise – fish and chips! Another drive, along a scenic route – in fact everywhere I saw was scenic.

One more stop – tea time! I still had a healthy appetite then – before food somehow became less important.

Afterwards we walked around another beautiful

village, Burley, buying the usual gifts from the unusual small shops. I loved it. Well tended gardens protected with grids and fences from the wild ponies. Animals, who, with the confidence of their ancestors, stopped motor and foot traffic alike. Some causing frustration, others excitement.

I love animals, if possible, more than flowers, so I was excited to see them. I learnt, from warning posters, many are killed by careless motorists, which made me sad. After all, they were here first.

It was early evening by the time we arrived back at the caravan. We played some games: draughts (not my favourite) but Beth enjoys it, and then several rounds of clock patience.

That night we should have slept well. We both went to bed happily tired and I soon fell asleep. But I immediately began to dream.

Most times in your life you never remember your dreams, in fact you usually don't even remember having any at all. Unless they are nightmares – those you cannot seem to forget.

This dream was different: It was so real and rather than struggling to wake up I found myself longing to stay asleep. Oddly I don't remember much about it, just I was not alone. There were other people moving around me. Though no one I could recognise. None of the loved and lost relatives, or friends, who you are usually said to meet in these twilight lands.

But I do remember how I felt, though it is impossible to describe. I have read quite a bit in my life, nothing clever, mainly romances or thrillers. I have also written many letters and kept my own diaries. But I could never put that feeling into words… It was overwhelming – in a good way. The nearest I could come to a description, was the feeling "all is right with the world." and something else. For the first time I knew what it felt like to be totally free.

I don't know what forced me out of this happiness, but suddenly I found myself in the dark. Really in the dark. It was like waking from a dream into a nightmare! Not just because of the sudden jolt from day to night, but because I felt trapped. Before I had always seen my body as a friend, perhaps more unreliable recently, but now it felt like the enemy. Like a prison.

I have seen babies when they are woken from a sound sleep. Their confusion makes them cross and weepy. As we grow up we sometimes get a return of that feeling, It's the aggravation you feel when you are dragged reluctantly from a satisfying slumber. Its what I felt now.

But I could move, because I must have got out of bed. The next thing I knew was dazzling light and seeing my Beth. She was the only thing I recognised. There certainly was nothing familiar in the kitchen around me.

For a moment I honestly didn't know where I was. I even thought I might be back in my dream, until Beth spoke and memory began to return.

My grand daughter took me back to bed, like a baby being placed back in its cot. I watched her waiting for me to fall asleep, and pretended to snore so she would return to her own room.

Eventually pretence became reality. It took a while – like a child on Christmas Eve, I was too excited to sleep. But I was disappointed: no more dreams came.

As it turned out it would be many nights before I repeated that wonderful experience.

The next morning the memory had faded, but I still felt in such high spirits I sang preparing breakfast. We continued our holiday. But something had changed.

When people know each other really well words become redundant. I knew Beth didn't want to discuss the subject, and so never brought it up.

It was the first time I had seen my Beth really frightened – it was in her eyes. Eyes that avoided looking directly into mine. But it wasn't fear for herself, it was for me.

How could I tell her I never felt more alive: had experienced a freedom I had never before known. My world had suddenly opened up beyond what I could presently see, and I wanted to see more.

Beth was the only one with whom I could have shared this secret. But I could not, mainly because I could not yet understand it myself. So how could I explain it to her? At best she would have thought I was hallucinating, at worst, going mad!

Maybe I should have tried – for her sake. So the coming years would have been less of a burden, less of this pointless guilt.

Nearly a decade on, I stand behind my grand daughter as she sits looking down at my empty, useless body, and I hope she is at last beginning to understand.

I am not there.

Chapter Three

Summer/Autumn/Winter 1983

ELIZABETH

The holiday ended, we returned home, and the day to day routine did seem to bring back a reassuring normalcy.

As the weeks, then months, passed, the fear gradually receded to the back of my mind.

But looks are deceptive and it is often when you are at your most complacent that fate has a habit of kicking you in the teeth.

In fact there was little relaxation in the next few months. Daily life become a balancing act. On one hand carrying on and keeping calm, on the other, tensed for any further episodes.

As it turned out there was little to worry about as the year progressed through summer and into autumn. There were no more night time disturbances, and I began to hope.

Of course there were other sorts of hiccups, but these could be written off as general forgetfulness.

It was so easy, too easy perhaps, to put incidents of absentmindedness down to the normal ageing process. These blips were even a cause for some humour. Sometimes laughter is the best antidote for fear.

One such was the incident of the iceberg lettuce. To be fair, this was not the sort of lettuce my grandmother was used to. Most of her experience with this well known salad ingredient was the traditional green and leafy variety.

At this point I still worked full time, but locally, so a short midday walk provided me with a substantial hot meal and Gran with company.

This had always been our routine. My succession of schools were within easy walking distance, so our main meal was lunch. Dinner was replaced by tea and supper.

This had two major advantages. It gave me more time at home with Gran, and spared me the ordeal of school dinners! I have no personal experience of such institutions, but heard enough first hand reports to prevent any envy.

No I was just grateful that somehow, either through accident or design, all my schools, and most of my employments, permitted lunch at home.

This particular lunch break I arrived home to be presented with a plate of lamb chops and mash served with a very strange, limp looking "cabbage." The taste, coupled with the disappearance of a lettuce I had bought for a prawn cocktail, soon solved the mystery.

We dined off the story for some time – which is more than we did with the wannabe cabbage!

Thank you my faithful diaries: I had forgotten how blessed a thing is laughter.

Without my scribbling I would have forgotten how many good times there were, even on difficult days. As the diaries progress there were certainly many more of those!

In later years I was fortunate to be able to transfer to freelance work, which allowed me to earn a living from home. Then, I now recall, we shared lunch time excursions to country pubs and many happy hours wandering around the gardens of stately homes. Each of these precious moments was thankfully immortalised in ink.

Autumn, with its inclement weather, appears to have brought an end to most outings that year.

Besides the preparations for Christmas soon took over. We began early, by necessity, since gift parcels had to be sent to America by the end of November. This meant we were present buying soon after Guy Fawkes Night.

You have to remember that this was in the days before Christmas cards appeared in the shops as soon as the school summer holidays ended!

Despite the long planning Christmas was always welcome in our home. Gran loved Christmas: young at heart, she never complained about the extra work or expense. Although cost was never a major part of our festivities. There was never any manic desperation to equate the pleasure it gave with the money we spent on it.

Once all the pre holiday office and pub binges ended, Christmas Day itself was quiet. But it was never grudgingly celebrated, nor depressing. It was a family event, and, OK, we might be a small one, but it was none the less special.

Besides we would often be joined by relatives or friends, because the one rule Gran had about

Christmas was that no one she knew would spent it alone. Surely, she declared, this was its real meaning: giving not taking.

In the afternoon, after the Queen's Speech, we gathered around the tree and opened our presents. It was a family tradition, and where it came from no one knows, but it proved a great success. It meant the usual anti climax following Christmas lunch was avoided, since everyone had something more to look forward to.

When I was younger Gran wisely knew a child expected some gift left by Father Christmas, so I always found a pillow case by my bedside. Yes, a pillow case: no stocking would have held the contents. These were always painstakingly wrapped annuals: Dandy, Beano and later Bunty. Gran was also shrewd enough to understand such presents would keep me occupied all morning.

A more recent, but no less important, addition to our Christmas day took place in the evening, between tea and supper. We all now gathered around the 'phone, while I dialled my mother and her family in the States. By this time, three thousand miles and five hours later, they were digesting their own turkey and trimmings.

It was a time for greetings, and thanks, as the receiver was handed around the members of each group. It also provided a chance to reminisce on Christmases past, the good old days. We were usually still laughing as we rang off. When we severed the connection there was never any sense of loss Any poignant thoughts were immediately dispelled by Gran with a suggestion of charades, and more food!

My last entry in this 1983 diary is, of course, New Year's Eve.

We were planning to stay up and celebrate at home. I had prepared the first footing items, which I would bring in after midnight. Yes, I know this should be a dark haired male, but I have learnt to be very flexible and politically correct in my superstitions.

As I close my little book I realise the last time it was open I was full of optimism and hope.

I had forgotten all about the unpredictability of fortune, and was totally unprepared for the blow approaching me.

BETSY

It was good to be home. Oh I enjoyed the holiday, but I have always been a homebody.

Besides, if I am truthful, I wanted more time on my own. I wanted Beth to feel everything was normal, and she could do that better at work. But my reasons were selfish too: I needed time to think, away from my grand daughter's watchful eyes.

As the days and weeks passed, there were no more dreams. I should have been content to forget, but I could not. Instead I spent every spare moment trying to replay my dream. Soon it became as difficult and distressing as trying to remember the face of a long gone loved one.

Maybe this obsession made me a little more forgetful, but I could laugh these lapses off, mainly because I had Beth as a willing accomplice. She wanted to believe it was simply a matter of old age, and, please forgive me – I let her.

It wasn't until the leaves began falling when I began to believe what I had experienced was exactly as it seemed to be – just a dream. Perhaps an unusually vivid one, but nevertheless just a one off glitch in my brain cells.

There's an old saying that if you stop looking for something you find will it.

How many times have you tried to remember something: a person's name, a film title, a place visited long ago, only to have it pop into your head when you least expect it?

Well that's exactly what happened. At the very moment I gave up asking for an answer it was given to me. I think its known as sod's law.

One evening just before Christmas I went to bed with every expectation of passing another uneventful night. Well unless awakened by a call of nature.

There was no reason to think otherwise. Nothing different had happened that day to set it apart. Thinking back, it was no more exciting or stressful than all the previous days. I could not even blame what happened on diet: not even a crumb of cheese had passed my mouth before bedtime.

But despite all signs to the contrary, as soon as my head hit the pillow I was asleep.

If any of you have experienced the effects of a general anaesthetic you will know what I am talking about. It is a strange, but not unpleasant, sensation. It is all in the single blink of an eye. The only difference being that instead of this "bat of an eyelid" taking me from pre-op to recovery, mine took me straight into my dream.

Although I don't think I can really call it a dream anymore. It would be like describing a diamond as glass. How can I hope to explain it? I have heard, with some doubt, people talk about near death experiences. In these visions they always seem to be walking in a white light. Well there was this most incredible brilliance, but it was full of colour. It was stunning but not blinding – in fact just the opposite. Suddenly everything became clear: and not just through my normal sight, hearing, taste, smell and feeling. If there is such a thing as a sixth sense, then that's as close as I can come to describing it.

Sometimes, over the years, I have experienced sensations which do not happen via my eyes, ears, tongue, nose, or skin. When these rare moments come it is as though they emerge from deep inside me.

I have never questioned what part of my body this feeling came from.

Perhaps I assumed it was the most complicated of mysteries: the brain.

But now I knew, as surely as I saw it set in stone, this "gift" did not come from my physical being at all.

Laugh at me if you like, I don't care, but for the want of another word let's call it "spirit" It was really clear to me now: when my body was at its weakest, this "spirit" was at its strongest.

The next morning my failing body was back in control, but it did not convince me any more that I am awaking from a dream.

There are countless things I don't grasp yet: which are still out of reach. But I know I am not deluded, or losing any marbles. Instead I am gaining something and, like most valuable objects, it does not come easily. Or without cost.

I have never really thought about death: not even when my husband died.

I have never desired, or feared, death, even with the prospect of meeting my dear George again. Because, although I have a strong bond to the idea of an afterlife, I have a stronger attachment to the reality of this life. I have my grand daughter.

I was, more than ever, determined to make the most of our life together, because somehow I knew how precious and brief our remaining time was.

Perhaps it was that sixth sense again. I certainly inherited some sort of intuition from my own grandmother, and I wonder if I have passed this on to Beth. I know she is nervous of the supernatural, because she makes fun of it.

In a moment of partial humour and total honesty I promised her I would never come back to haunt her.

In the last years I have had many misgivings about making this promise – but maybe there is another way. A way which I am not yet strong enough to carry out.

Meanwhile there are moments for laughter and closeness: like our weekly pension trips to the post office and our drives out to a country pub for lunch.

But it is harder to stay in this world when the other is becoming more and more fascinating.

Now it is I who feel guilty for looking forward to these nightly escapes. Yes, they have become as regular as night following day.

For now that's how it remained: two separate, clearly defined worlds. But all was about to change, and that's when our lives really became complicated and cruel.

Chapter Four

March 1984

ELIZABETH

Early in spring Gran tripped over the kitchen step, and fell forward: hitting her head and arm. The latter was more spectacular, since a sharp door lock sliced through the flesh and created a deep and messy gash just below the elbow. However a few well placed stitches dealt with minimum trauma. It was the head injury which caused the most concern to the doctor.

I had been taking advantage of an unseasonably warm spring and hanging out some washing, when I heard first the commotion of a door banging. A few moments later I heard Gran's cry for help. But those few moments could have covered a short, but life threatening, loss of consciousness, and it was this which worried the doctor.

Therefore an hospital visit was advised, which would include an overnight stay until they could assess the extent of any damage: physical or mental.

Gran hated hospitals following two negative experiences. That both took place in her youth just added to her fear, since most phobias only increase given time and imagination.

All of this, combined with medication, had an extreme, but hardly surprising effect. She became disorientated and reverted to the helpless state I remembered from our holiday. This time she never completely recovered.

It was hard saying goodbye when I left her. She was well enough to get out of bed, but not come home, and I remember waving to her from the car park.

I experienced some horrible déjà vu at that moment: as I saw that small forlorn figure through that high hospital window.

It was many years ago, when I was a child, but none the less harrowing for that. My grandmother always took me to primary school and always waited by the school gate until the bell rang and I went in. On this one occasion she left just before our last wave, and I was so distressed I ran down the hill from the playground and followed her home.

So watching that small figure above me I knew exactly how she felt because I had been there: she was lonely and helpless, but she couldn't follow me home.

I slept badly, and when I did it was filled with dreams. Not nightmares, no monsters chasing me as I tried to escape in slow motion.

Instead, it was I pursuing some unknown goal, but never getting any closer. When I woke up it was to the sound of ringing. Still half asleep, and fully exhausted, I groped for the bedside 'phone. From the other end of the line I heard a ward nurse suggesting I collect Gran as soon as possible. It was eight o'clock in the morning. Apparently I was not the only one who had passed a disturbed night!

I was so relieved to get her home, although

probably not as thankful as the hospital staff to get rid of her. Her restlessness had kept the whole ward awake, disturbing her fellow patients and frustrating their carers. It was 2am before she had fallen into a deep sleep: whether by nature or medication was never revealed.

So once more Gran came home, but this time there was no longer any possibility for pretence. Increasingly her short term memories disappeared and she lived in those of the past. I could not blame her: they were probably much happier times. I only wished I had the opportunity and energy to do the same.

Instead, for me, it was like a steady, relentless drip wearing me away.

Before I reached the point of lethargic acceptance I went to our GP, who dismissed it as old age. In fact my direct question "is this senile dementia" received the firm and authoritative response "no."

What I did not know then, but learnt later, was after I left the surgery he wrote down a different diagnosis – Alzheimer's. What was in his mind, what were his motives? Maybe he just felt helpless, and I know everyone, but doctors especially, hate that feeling. But he was our first line of defence, and he failed.

It wasn't until the last months of her life, when another practitioner dealt with a severe, and messy, bowel infection, we found out about this earlier verdict.

I cannot say I don't blame that first GP. Perhaps he thought he was being compassionate, but we all know where good intentions lead to.

Certainly the following years became some sort of Hell for me. No, too much misery came from that decision.

So I was left to my own ends. I was in no position to identify the problem: in fact by 1985 I was already being carried along in the drowning torrent which can overwhelm most carers. It was a case of just keeping my head above water and coping with every new burden trying to drag me down.

There have been improvements in support and treatment in the last few years: but even in those days we could have set the wheels in motion for respite care and financial aid.

As it was both only came in the last six months, when the new GP called in psychiatric expertise for home assessment. By this time Gran had completely reverted, not so much to second childhood, as second infancy. She just sat on the floor while the therapist asked simple questions, which she didn't understand – let alone provide a rational answer.

She was classified as 'off the chart' for assessment purposes.

At last the support service went into action. It was a case of too little, too late.

By the Christmas of 1992 Gran had only three months to live.

BETSY

Hospital was where my new life really began. It's where, for the first time, I met fellow travellers and through them learnt so much more about our new world.

Until then I had felt release, while still tied by some invisible cord to my body.

At first I had been anxious about letting it out of my sight. Like a nervous toddler clinging to its mother: I was wary of what lay beyond, and terrified of being lost.

As time went by and knowledge grew, I came to understand it was time to start letting go. My stay in hospital was the beginning of this insight.

But in the spring of 1984 all I felt was frustration, and even anger, at the emotional strain this "tug of war" caused. I am afraid that Beth saw my transformation from an easy going Gran, to a cantankerous old codger, as proof of my unhappiness. She could not have been more wrong!

It was only when I escaped that I was truly happy. My only regret was how much distress this caused Beth. It was my struggle she must have seen when I waved her goodbye that night in hospital. She looked so small and lost down in the car park that it broke my heart. Deep down within my new self I knew this was the start of a long goodbye.

When I later went to sleep, I didn't care the bed

was uncomfortable, and the people around me were strangers. I just hoped none of this affected my ability to 'dream.'

Sorry, but I still do not have another word which adequately describes my experience to you of this world. What does pure sensation have to do with sense and reason. We, for now, are literally worlds apart!

For some time sleep would not come, and I know I was a right pain in the backside! Tossing, turning and moaning away to myself – it's a wonder I wasn't certified then and there! Finally some "angel of mercy" gave me a drink, which I suspect was laced with some medication, and off I drifted

Oh, of course, all you 'doubting Thomass' out there will claim some sort of drug induced hallucination, but I know what I saw. I just KNOW it, and I am so certain I don't care about proving it. You will know in your own good time.

Suddenly I found myself looking down at the body I had known so well: tried to protect and cherish for so many years. It now meant nothing to me beyond a mild interest: is that what I look like to other people: is that what I look like to Beth?

Strangely enough I felt no connection at all. It wasn't somewhere I wanted to be any more, it wasn't loved, it wasn't hated – it just wasn't important. I suddenly saw it for what it was – a ruin which had become old, shabby and redundant. A condemned building, and one I was happy to walk away from.

Without Beth to consider that's exactly what I did.

But this was my first time, so I was still cautious

and didn't intend to venture very far. So I took my first toddler steps down the ward, passed the "guards," and straight out the door. This in itself gave a real sense of power. Such establishments probably do not mean to be intimidating, but they have every advantage to succeed. They even have their own prison tags which prevent you escaping!

Yes I know they are wonderful places with some marvellous people, and I have reason to be grateful for them. But I also have my reasons to be wary: my experience of all things medical has not been good. Control issues are one of them.

Hospitals are indeed the best places to be ill, they are also the worst.

At the time you are your most vulnerable they make you feel even more helpless. I don't think it is intentional, but, like most institutions, giving general order takes away personal independence. That's probably why I never liked school either!

So, it was with a naughty child's pleasure I stepped through the door and left. Yes I do mean stepped through. I had already learnt that accepted rules of behaviour did not apply here.

I found myself in a corridor: familiar from a trip to the X-ray department. Then it appeared dark, and intimidating, now it was bright and welcoming. This was odd, because it was only lit by a low, night time, lighting.

But no longer was there anything here which could affect or hurt me. This was a world without the power to cause physical pain or discomfort. I felt so safe, so untouchable. I felt larger than life, as if all those senses released from my body, had multiplied ten fold in my new "psychic" (again for want of a better word) state.

For no reason at all, except instinct or preference, I turned right and walked into a nurse who was planning to enter the door I had just come through. In fact I literally did walk "into" her – and out the other side. She appeared to register absolutely nothing – not even the shiver supposed to accompany humans touching spirits. I, on the other hand, felt so much! Shock at my first such encounter, but something else – I felt her. Or rather her spirit. For a brief moment, I connected with that mysterious being which is part of us all.

If drowning people "see" their past life flash before them, then that's what I "saw." But it wasn't my life it was hers, and as I passed through her, it passed through me, None of it made much sense – too quick, like rewinding an old film. Call it what you will. Take your pick, from the misfiring of a disturbed brain to the simple truth, but in those seconds I saw her soul.

I firmly believe none of us are perfect. In fact it is the mixture of light and shade which makes us so interesting, but when that balance is out then the result is either an angel or devil. In this instance I knew this person was in the wrong job: she had power without conscience. She was not a good person, and I felt sorry for her patients.

"Right bitch isn't she" this statement came from a woman standing directly opposite me: on the other side of the corridor. This was definitely a night for surprises!

Before I recovered enough to agree, she

continued, "Don't worry you're not going round the bend – I heard we have a new 'waiter'." Whoever she was, she wasn't very polite, or patient, because she interrupted my intended reply again!

But, in fact, she was a patient because she wore the same practical, but unflattering, easy access, gown I was wearing.

What the hell was she doing out of bed at this hour – but, on the other hand, I was in no position to criticize!

Even more to the point "how could she see me?"

Of course there was only one answer and she gave it – "I know: I can see you because I'm a waiter too."

At last I got a word in edgeways enough to repeat "waiter?"

She gave me the warmest smile and explained, "It's what we call ourselves around here – as a sort of joke. This is "God's waiting room – get it?" Then she added, in another one of her question statements, "Shall we go for a walk?" Without giving my agreement, or her expecting one, we set off down the right hand corridor. It was a short journey, but an instructive one.

During it most of my unspoken queries were answered.

First of all I learnt about my companion. She introduced herself as Joan, and she was indeed a fellow patient. She, or rather her body, was in a coma and she had been wandering this hospital for some time. She didn't know exactly how long because time meant nothing. Eavesdropping on her carers and visitors she understood she had suffered some sort of stroke. She was about that age: she looked in her late sixties.

Let me explain straight away that Joan was not one of those see through apparitions depicted by films or captured by ghost hunters. She was as solid as you or me (well perhaps not me at the moment) – in fact more real than mere flesh and blood.

She was also remarkably lively for one in her condition, and very chatty. It was from her that I found out about "God's waiting room."

Some people learn from experience, others from books, but for me the best way of all was a good teacher. The good teachers are those who are not possessive of their own knowledge. The great teachers are those who share this knowledge and then encourage their students to surpass them. Joan was a great teacher.

But where was she taking me?

This soon became clear as we turned into a side ward and she began, what I later learnt, were her 'rounds.'

The small room was crowded: there were at least six people sitting and standing around a bed. The bed was lit by a spotlight which gave just enough illumination to see a small figure, painfully thin and horribly pale. It was a young child, one who would not live to celebrate another birthday.

My human heart would have brought tears to my old eyes, but my new vision had opened up another possibility. No longer did I have to imagine an eternity of nothingness for this little soul. There was something beyond – after all I was part of it, wasn't I?

Perhaps these people felt the same way: maybe they had somehow managed to hold onto their faith, because here there was no fear or despair. Sadness, of course, but beyond and above that – love.

The quietness was only broken by a soft feminine voice, the child's mother.

She sat on the bed, stroking the little forehead and talking so slowly that I could not catch a word. It didn't matter – words were unnecessary.

Suddenly she stopped, slid onto the bedcover besides her daughter (for it was a little girl) and cuddled her so tenderly As if such a gentle touch could hurt her. But just as a mother's love had cradled her into this world, now it helped her leave it. I saw the mother hold her own breath for a few seconds, as if she intended to follow her. She then gave a little gasp of pure pain and began to cry.

At her side I saw a child, who could have been a healthy twin, but was not.

This young girl was trying hard to console her mother, but could not. Joan knelt down, whispered something to the child, took her hand and led her towards me.

"This is Katherine" she said "and she wants to go home."

I took the vacant hand that Katherine held out and together we all went through the door into the corridor.

As we walked Joan explained, "Children handle it much better: they are more innocent and open minded."

Well I couldn't let that go without an argument,

"But this is so wrong – what did this child, or her parents, do to be punished like this – it's so unfair!"

Joan had a response she had probably repeated patiently many times, "I could say life isn't fair, but actually it is. Its people who aren't. And why do you suppose this is punishment. You are old enough to know that bad things happen to good people and vice versa. It isn't the divine hand of God handing out rewards and retribution – it's the joy and misery of free will.

You just need to look at it a different way. Oh I used to think like you, but hanging around here has taught me many things. The most important being humility – I still, and probably never will, know everything. That's what blind faith is about – and its natural to the young of any species – until we teach them differently.

I know one thing for certain though – the younger they are the easier it seems to be for them. I think its because they haven't had time to lose trust.

They haven't been tainted by the world, or" she added, " become too attached to its possessions."

We stopped, and I could see no reason why. I was just about to open my mouth, and probably once more put my foot in it, when I saw someone appear down the corridor.

Joan whispered to me "Stay here" and took Katherine to meet the oncoming figure. As they met they appeared to merge. Oh yes I can hear you sceptics claiming it was a mere a trick of the light. But I probably lost you anyway back at the "out of body" bit!

A few moments later only Joan returned, with a

brief answer to my unspoken question – "Katherine's grandmother." Now this sort of conversation, if not part of a comedy routine, can be downright annoying, but somehow with Joan you got used to it. It wasn't as if she was pre-empting your words, more as if she knew what you were thinking – because she had been there before you.

"She didn't seem upset or bothered at all to leave her family" I said the thought out loud, and then felt guilty as it appeared to sound critical. Joan simply replied, "I told you children are different – unspoilt – they don't understand our meaning of the word 'goodbye.' To them it just means 'see you later.' Besides she IS with her family."

So began my re-education.

Over the next months I returned to the hospital and Joan, not only every night but increasingly during the day. I knew our time together was limited and wanted to learn as much as I could. I was aware that any moment she could disappear, either back to one life or on to the next.

Little did I know then, I was not only her student, but her successor.

Chapter Five

October 1985

ELIZABETH

Eighteen months have gone by since the hospital visit.

It was only one night, but it was enough. Enough to begin a long agonizing process. One of growing isolation for both of us.

At first it appeared, when Gran returned from hospital, so did her memory.

She certainly recognised her home and her grand daughter. This was one blessing. Even in the last months of her life, although she barely knew where she was, she always remembered me. Remembered yes, but did she really know me. Did she look at me sometimes with suspicion, as though I had changed. In short did she look at me as a stranger – as I sometimes looked at her?

How else can I explain what was soon to happen – how she would be so easily manipulated. That the perpetrator was another close family member just added to the sense of betrayal. That's when my pain and loneliness reached a whole new level – when I lost all trust.

But this event was for the future, and we could still put up some sort of barrier against the truth.

Although Gran became more and more forgetful and confused, our routine temporarily kept us on track. There were a few wobbles and some interesting variations at lunchtime, which were often raw or overcooked, but we generally muddled on. Though I took the precaution of never buying iceberg lettuce.

One thing, I always had a substantial breakfast. Gran was an early bird, and always got up to prepare this hot meal. I encouraged this as long as I could: it was part of our crucial routine. Although probably not the healthiest diet, I thought it gave Gran a feeling of purpose in a world from which, even before her Alzheimer's, she was becoming alienated.

Her generation probably witnessed the most change of any other before or since. She narrowly missed being a Victorian, being born just a few years after the queen's death. She lived through the turmoil and strain of two world wars and one cold one. When she was born there was barely any technology, and none which affected the working classes – of which she was proudly part. By the time she died you could not escape it, even if you wanted to and most people did not. It certainly took a lot of drudgery out of domestic labour, and provided hours of channelled entertainment to occupy the freed time.

From the beginning though we traded much of our humanity for an easier life.

We gave up a lot of natural abilities in exchange for "progress": imagination for one and sensitivity for another. Hi tech virtual reality games leave very little scope for the imagination, and being bombarded with real images of worldwide death and destruction tends to numb your compassion.

I am looking down now at one casualty of the technological revolution: the written word. My diary.

I turn it over in my hands and am immediately struck by how solid it feels and suddenly realise how precious this little book is. It is many years old but it is as real as when it was put away. It satisfies the senses: touch and sight are obvious. It has no voice but speaks to us, for you hear the words as you read them. And who has never noticed the distinctive aroma of fresh print, or old paper. Of course there is no taste in the usual meaning, but books do appeal to a sense of taste: but of the brain not the tongue.

All of this in the plain, and complex, object in my hands.

I doubt any emails will survive so long, or be so treasured. Reading these, my most private thoughts, written in my own hand, I recall just how far we descended from those moments captured in 1985.

So hard to read. But if you have the time and energy of hindsight you realise the cleverness and cruelty of such diseases. It sneaks up on you. If the full impact was dumped on you from day one, you would refuse to cope. As it is the slow process slowly crushes you – like some accused heretic being pressed to death – one stone at a time.

At first it was just little things: forgetting the time, days of the week: by October 1985 it was my birthday. I wasn't surprised; to be truthful I had almost missed it myself, until cards began arriving.

Gran was slipping away from me – I noticed that she slept more; not just at night but during the day, which probably explains the hit and miss lunches.

This became clear over the Christmas holidays and prompted a rare New Year resolution.

Short term I could probably enlist the help of a friendly neighbour; most of my friends were occupied in their own employment, and most of Gran's were too old – or dead. So I was looking for a long term solution. Luckily I was working in publishing, which gave plenty of opportunity for part-time or freelance work.

So I turn the pages and reach the end of another diary – another year.

It was a year which would bring some tough decisions. Making them would begin to isolate us both, but I was running out of the luxury of choice.

BETSY

Last spring, before Joan led me back to my ward, she told me her belief, or philosophy, if you prefer. It was a simple one.

Be useful. Be good to others. Hence her "rounds" – every time she sensed someone was dying in the hospital she went to them, and if required, helped them come to terms. Most did not need her help, in which case she stood back and watched them happily pass by to a place they had come to believe was non existent. The majority just needed a little guidance. But there were some who were too tied to this world.

When I had asked what happened to them, Joan became quiet as she answered, "Usually persuasion and the reality of their situation work, but a few choose to stay. Perhaps they are attached to people or places through unresolved issues. Sometimes it's love, more often its revenge.

Joan didn't tell me that first night, but there was a third group. I was to learn about them later. If there was such a thing as limbo then they were caught in it, and at the risk of being judgemental – they deserved it!

But for the moment there was so much to do: for a practical start I needed to learn how to travel around. Tomorrow night I would be back home and it was a long walk to the hospital!

It was quite easy really, once you got the hang

of it. You simply visualised where you wanted to be, and blink of an eye, you were there.

So the next evening, when I had finally mastered my new means of transportation, Joan was already waiting for me. She stood where we had first met: outside my old ward.

I had given up questioning the method and extent of her powers. Perhaps she was some sort of spiritual air traffic controller: using psychic radar to plot and track the movement of all incoming travellers!

But there was no time for further speculation. Without any preamble she started walking off in the opposite direction to the previous night – down the corridor to the left. While I hurried to catch up with her, she explained that last night had been a 'quiet' one. Tonight, apparently, we already had a 'client' waiting.

So we were beginning our "rounds" with a summons to A & E. From the state of the injuries resuscitation was already a lost cause, but the medics did their best, even though their patient would not have appreciated it!

Apparently it was a suicide – and not the first attempt – according to the paramedics. An earlier more common drug overdose having failed, he had climbed to the top of a multi storey car park and jumped. This was obviously not just a cry for help.

John, as the paramedics introduced the patient to his doctors, was already looking down at his own mangled corpse when we arrived.

Fortunately, for me, it appears the spirit does not retain the damage from its body, because the 'soul' before us was a thankfully intact and handsome young man.

Joan gently asked him to follow her and, without any question or argument, he walked by her side. We left just before death was pronounced.

I followed behind this time as I did not think I should be part of their conversation, but had many questions of my own. I was not a Catholic but surely suicide was a taboo in most modern religions. Isn't it an unforgivable offence against God to cut short what he has given? Would there be anyone to meet him? Or would he be despatched into some nether region of everlasting fire and brimstone? Did I really want to know?

By the time we reached the corridor where I had last seen Katherine I wasn't sure I wanted the answers.

In fact as I turned the corner into the long hallway there was not one person waiting – but a welcoming party! Joan and her companion had already reached them, so I saw the group surround and embrace him before they joined into one encircling glow.

When Joan rejoined me I asked, before she could interrupt, "But I thought suicides were held in some sort of purgatory."

It was the first time I had seen Joan angry, but I understood it was not directed at me: "don't you think they have suffered enough in this world?"

Then she said more gently "this is a waiting room, not a courtroom."

She continued, almost to herself, "Perhaps it was a mistake for us to put God in our image – we have transferred our own petty prejudices and hypocrisies. God, whatever, he or she, is, is not callous or malicious and cannot be judged by our own flawed standards." To further make her point, she quoted an often glib, but always appropriate piece of advice "Judge not, lest ye be judged,"

I had obviously touched a raw nerve because Joan had not finished. "It is the same with animals: why do so many religions refuse them souls? What arrogant mind would believe their creator would fashion the most innocent of creatures without a soul." Then she seemed to recall my presence and concluded, " Most animals have a hard enough time in this world without denying them a kinder afterlife."

There was nothing more I could say, but as I came to know Joan over time I learnt that she had been heavily involved with animal shelters for many years. So at the time I thought this was just a case of wishful thinking. It wasn't until Joan had gone I discovered it was in fact the simple truth. Souls are not the preserve of humanity.

That night there was one more death. It was a 92 year old woman, Mary, whose demise would have been considered "natural" had she not been kept alive for several days following a stroke. She had been wandering around the hospital since admission, and met us outside her screened off cubicle with the eager greeting "is it time?"

Joan just smiled and nodded.

"Thank goodness, I have been so bored, and I want to see my husband, it's been such a long time. He died in the Great War you know – Somme." We took our usual route, while she talked excitedly. Almost as if she had returned to a day at the beginning of this century: a young girl on her wedding day.

As we reached our destination she turned to

us both and asked "how do you stand this waiting around?" But as she turned back she had forgotten her question. This time there was no need to accompany her further. She saw the figure of a young man waiting for her and actually ran towards him. And as she ran, I swear to God, by the time she reached him she was that young bride once more.

We were both silent as we walked back: no words were adequate or necessary. Although Joan must have experienced many such reunions, it was an encounter which, I suspect, never left you unaffected.

When our choked throats allowed us to speak, Joan announced,

"Well that's it for tonight – now I have other people for you to meet."

This time I followed her in yet another direction and down several flights of stairs. It did briefly pass my mind how strange it was not to worry about missing a step and falling, how wonderful it was to exist without fear.

It didn't even bother me when I saw the sign on the door we approached.

Generally the idea of entering a morgue, especially at night, is a definite spine chiller, but I was just fascinated. What were we doing here, and what sort of people hang around a morgue?

Well not the sort usually associated with such macabre places: no vampires, or mad scientists looking for spare parts. In fact I was introduced to the most agreeable and spirited (pun intended) group of characters. Although, unlike the bodies around us, none of them were actually dead.

Like most groups of people there were all sorts:

representing gender, age, race. But in this instance all of these divisions were irrelevant. Let me introduce them to you as they were introduced to me.

Even in these circumstances politeness was the order of the night, so it was ladies first. Sarah, was a fellow coma patient following a car accident. She had extensive head injuries, and although only in her mid twenties had already reached the acceptance stage. Listening in on consultations with her parents she knew the reality of recovery and had come to terms with death. Of course this decision was made easier by the newly found conviction that this was not the end!

She was a lively, sensible, young woman, and although she regretted all those missed opportunities in life; she also accepted the truth. The state of her body's physical condition meant most of these choices were already lost. She also disproved the theory that young people are basically selfish, because her main concern was the effect of her continued existence on her parents. I liked her so much – probably because she was a younger version of my Beth.

There were no more ladies so Joan moved to the youngest male: probably because he stood next to Sarah. A case of the young gravitating towards the young, as some form of mutual comfort. Or perhaps because Sarah's spirit was just as attractive as her body had been.

Whatever the reason James was a quiet teenager, who left all explanation to Joan. Perhaps he felt embarrassed because, despite coming from a loving family, he had made bad decisions and chosen dangerous company. A deadly combination which left him in a coma following a drug overdose.

Unlike Sarah he still hoped to return and make up with his parents. He wanted the chance to start again. This showed because he was not at peace with his situation. There was no anger – he had never moved on from denial. I liked him too, but my overwhelming feeling was pity. I hoped that some compassionate force would send him back.

It seems pointless to talk about age in our shared condition, but this mental journal of mine must cater for you bodied people.

The final two members of our small "club" were both elderly and currently sedated by morphine, being in the later stages of cancer. Curiously such words here have no sense of fear or awkwardness, they are mere explanations – they do not matter, only as a means of conversation.

Jack and Robert (who preferred Bob) were looking forward to moving on.

Both of them had more connections to the next life than they did to this. Yes they did have grieving families gathered around hushed hospital beds, but they missed the loved ones who had gone before them. There were wives, siblings and friends who had waited patiently and a reunion was long overdue.

Finally Joan made my introduction and a general rush of questions began – all except James, who stood quietly back just listening. Perhaps he reasoned that by failing to acknowledge our group he would not join it. He stood like a polite child, being seen but not heard. In fact that's exactly what he was, and I hoped he would get his second chance.

I was confused, but not because of James reluctance, or the others' excitement. There was someone else hovering around us – well not literally hovering, but pacing around us trying to interrupt our chatter. What made it even stranger was that this rude gatecrasher was not a young child, but a middle aged businessman, complete with pin striped suit.

Most of our party ignored him, but Joan took this intruder aside. I tried to catch their exchange, but, without being bad-mannered to my new friends, it was impossible. Shortly after their discussion he left.

Later when Joan and I were alone I asked who this man was. She explained he was a sort of visitor: christened by us "waiters" as an "out of body tourist."

She advised me to either ignore them, or, as she had done, suggest they return to their body. Either they would be jolted back into it, or pass on.

I asked if she would be called to attend if the latter. She said "You will understand eventually that most people pass on quite naturally. The tunnel of light, you have heard about, is real. In our physical world it is usually dismissed as a brain malfunction: but, in fact, there is no more evidence to disprove than there is to support it. You have seen a glimpse of it yourself in the form of 'the greeters'- our name for those from the other side." I must have looked a little vague, because she made it clearer "The figures in the corridor." Then she added with a smile "Unless I am a brain malfunction too."

Joan carried on "At the moment of bodily death, I understand – since I have never experienced it myself, the released spirit sees this tunnel of light and is just drawn into it. Sort of like a moth to a flame, or, "another smile, "someone being sucked out of a decompressed plane window."

Now I had seen such an event recreated in one of my grand daughter's videos. In this instance it had been a rather large character, and as he was also the villain, it provided more humour than horror, so I could understand and share this visual joke.

She continued "Anyway most of the time I am redundant, but there are enough exceptions to the rule to keep me busy."

If I had spirit eye brows I must have raised them, because Joan shed a bit more light "Usually I am here to help fellow 'waiters' come to terms with their situation: most are short term, like Katherine, a few are long term, like yourself.

The long term are special, but we will go into that some other time."

I completely missed the significance of this remark in my eagerness to voice a question. "What about John, the suicide?" I blurted out before realising this would probably offend Joan. She either chose to ignore my blunder, or was relieved I had not picked up on her last remark. "Sometimes, when people pass suddenly, even when it's planned, it's a shock. Suicides are usually desperate to escape this life, not eager for the next. That's why it's so pointless, not to mention cruel, to condemn them in the afterlife. It won't stop them, because if they feel damned in this world, why would they care about what's beyond it? Their greatest hope is an eternity of oblivion, and, increasingly in our 'enlightened' modern society, that's all which is offered."

Some scenic train of thought made me ask Joan if she knew what would happen to Sarah and James. She said not and I believed her, there was no reason to lie. As it turned out I would be around to see for myself when that question was answered.

I also learnt the answer to a question unasked then: why I was special? For one thing: there was no other person like myself at the hospital.

We are rare at general hospitals because most of us are found in nursing homes or long term psychiatric establishments. People suffering from Alzheimer's, senile dementia, call it what you will, are usually placed into separate institutions. They used to be called asylums – a word with a personal history for me. One which, even now, gives me a sense of sadness and guilt.

My own grandmother was committed to an asylum for the last years of her life, and the memory of those visits still haunts me. In the late 1930s little had changed since Victorian times, including the name. Thankfully I wasn't aware of the barbaric experimental treatments being carried out. but I was witness to the terrible conditions.

I remember my once immaculate grandmother sitting, in strange clothes, amidst the squalor of an overcrowded dirty ward. Other patients shuffled around her muttering obscenities and performing all sorts of lewd behaviour. It must have been like some sort of Hell for her.

I have seen it before: how people suffering from mental illness can become aggressive and violent. I began to wonder if something takes over our vacant bodies – like a possession. I must have spoken the thought because Joan interrupted my mental wanderings with the response "no". Joan expanded her short reply by saying most people in our halfway house (I prefer this to limbo) are attached to their bodies by their families. Ironically it is love which creates this push and pull predicament.

That's why so many are angry. They are tore between emotional physical ties and the freedom they experience here. It makes them frustrated by the claustrophobia of their own bodies, and a little resentful of their carers, who are unsuspectingly gaolers.

It is no fluke the patients in nursing homes are much calmer. It isn't so much the effects of medication as the fact there is no clash of interests.

Most of the time they are, literally, not all there. Put even more simply, they are free to be free.

So why did I end up here? If I had not fallen over, if I had not ended up in hospital, if I had not been prepared by my earlier experience. Too many ifs. I am not sure, if, up until then, I believed in coincidence or not.

Afterwards there was no doubt – there is no such thing as an accident, lucky or otherwise.

There is always a plan.

Chapter Six

September 1986

ELIZABETH

Another long year later and so much, yet so little, has changed.

The changes are subtle: you cannot measure them by days or weeks, but they are no less significant, just less obvious. At least it seems that way.

People, who I thought knew me so well, do not seem to notice my increasing desperation. Just occasionally, usually in the darkness of the night, a sense of isolation overwhelms me. Then I cry, although not for long.

I don't have the energy to waste, and exhaustion replaces the lullaby which years ago once soothed me back to sleep.

Sometimes my restless brain travels back to that past. A time which Gran seems to inhabit more and more. It seems to give her pleasure, but it's a journey I try not to make because it is too painful. The time may come when such memories may provide comfort, but not yet.

To be fair to my family and friends I was a good actor. My family were too far away to discover the truth of the situation, and the latter too easily deceived by my determination to cope. We are indeed sometimes our own worst enemy!

Why do we do this? Is it a fear of failure; or just dealing with what we cannot change – stiff upper lip syndrome?

In any case we are all guilty of some degree of self absorption. Who has never given a promise, in a moment of pure benevolence, they have later regretted. We are all human and life goes on: sometimes it passes us by.

That's what seemed to be happening to me at the moment. I was still working, but through necessity rather than pride or fulfilment. Certainly not human companionship, since my office was also now my home. A mixed blessing, but nonetheless one which provided financial support.

Gran's state pension would barely cover necessities and besides her money was her independence. We kept to what routine we could, and on pension day the weekly post office queue was followed by a grocery shopping trip.

But I never expected her to contribute to any household bills or repairs, and what she did with her money was her business. Although I do sometimes speculate what secrets her bedroom floorboards may hide.! But, difficult as it may be to understand, I had no interest in how she disposed of her money. It was simply a matter of fairness. She had looked after me then: now it was my turn.

This unspoken agreement stemmed from her stories of the Depression and a close shave with the dreaded "means test." A degrading and heartbreaking policy whereby government officials could enter your home and sell possessions to pay your unemployment benefit.

As a legacy of this experience she always viewed saving, not as the miserly acquisition of wealth, but as a safety net. Never again did she want to be at the whim of someone else's generosity or greed.

Gran always led by example and, even before I knew what money was, she set me up with a Post Office savings account. It was as unthinkable for me to take Gran's pension as it would have been for her to raid my childhood piggy bank!

But not all people are the same, and I was shortly to learn that lesson from bitter experience.

Luckily I didn't have time to worry about the future – even when it was only a few months away. My 1986 diary is evidence of my state of mind: it is short, sharp and badly written. Each messy entry is proof my life was becoming, as the Good Book says " sufficient unto the day is the evil thereof." Or in my translation "live just one day at a time."

Sometimes I wonder if I am going mad too: most of the time I don't have the time, or energy to worry about it. I had other concerns to occupy my mind.

Working with children is hard work, and Gran was reverting more and more to childhood behaviour. With the young in body there is the consolation that although they may get worse they will eventually get better. With the young in mind there is only the certainty they will just get worse.

One of these relapses was a tendency to rude frankness. Such innocent candour may be tolerated, even charming, in young children, but to have your deficiencies proclaimed loudly by a white haired grandmother is just embarrassing. One such friend, on being offered the guests customary cup of tea and cream cake, was greeted by the comment: "God you're getting fat." Needless to say it was a short visit, and the cake went untouched!

Those friends who did not stop visiting of their own volition soon found less invitations forthcoming, and I suspect were secretly relieved.

My world was getting smaller and smaller. The walls which had once formed a loving home were closing in around me. My protective sanctuary was now a prison cell. Without access to respite care all I could do was retreat into a corner. I would have been depressed – had I the time!!!

As it was, increasingly I was alone. All my life I had had the strength of Gran's support, now those foundations were slipping away. I had never felt so helpless, or alone, before.

As with depression it was hard to find any joy in the present, or see any hope for the future. Did I see any brighter prospects? Certainly my diary entries don't give any indication of this: they are filled with gloom and doom – if I bothered writing at all! For the first time since I learnt to write and began these journals, there are blanks in the pages.

Little did I know then there are worst things than feeling isolated. Until that autumn I was living under a beautiful illusion, namely although things were bad I was not truly alone. I had a family, and as green summer leaves began to rust, I at last felt something I had forgotten – hope.

My mother was arriving for her annual visit, and bringing relief with her. She had written ahead to suggest a temporary solution to my predicament. She would look after her mother, while I took a much needed respite.

Those diary entries, which anticipate and plan a holiday with an old school friend, should recall a sense of happiness and relief. They do not. In fact I remember nothing about that break, not even where we went.

I paid heavily for that one week of forgotten pleasure. The next six years of my life were lived in the reality of previously unimagined loneliness, and with a betrayal I have never been able to forgive or forget.

Would it have been better to retain my illusions, to remain in ignorance? I do not know.

All I do know is at the time it was a blessing – an answer to my prayers.

An old well worn piece of advice comes to mind: "Be careful what you ask for!"

BETSY

Another year and where has the time gone?

Why is it the bad days seem endless while the good ones disappear so quickly. My only sorrow is while my own time speeds by, I know my grand daughter's life has become a long daily grind.

I have added guilt to this regret, because I am spending more and more time at the hospital It's been a busy time there – especially since Joan's departure.

She has been gone about three months now, but she taught me so much before she left.

For one thing I have learnt that I do not have to stay anywhere for long: with a little concentration and imagination the world is my oyster. Practice makes perfect and, over the last year I have become quite good at "bobbing" around.

At first the novelty of my new skill would have wasted much valuable time, again had it not been for Joan.

As I think I said before, she is one of those precious people who are born teachers. Someone whose gentle, wise words, draw you to them like metal to a magnet. She taught me patience and that I will have all the time in the world to satisfy my itchy feet. Later. But, for now, my place is here, in this hospital. I have a job to do. What's more, what is so wonderful: my work has become my pleasure.

I find such happiness in the proof it is indeed "more blessed to give than receive," and amazement in the irony that by giving you receive more!

So began my apprenticeship. It was not to be a long one – Joan and I had little enough time together on this earth. The fact we enjoyed each other's company, and our work, meant those months disappeared quickly, too quickly.

During this time I have found out why I am special. Why I was chosen.

There is always a plan, and part of this was my transformation – from a "waiter" to a "guide."

Most fellow "waiters" are short term, like Jack and Bob, and both have long since passed on. In fact they died within hours of each other. Families surrounding them with such selfless love they were content to let them go.

Once permanently released from their failing bodies they drifted by us with a brief farewell smile, towards a light we could not see. Beautiful deaths, but not ones which need a "guide."

Neither do those drifting between coma and beyond like Sarah and James.

Sarah passed on shortly after Jack and Bob.

She was reconciled, even eager, to begin her "awfully big adventure": We had not spent much time talking, but enough to learn that a childhood favourite had been "Peter Pan." Her parents had read through it many times at her bedside: in the hope of giving encouragement or peace. I like to think those inspired words by J M Barrie provided both.

It was time to go: goodbyes had been said many times in the past weeks.

When Sarah returned to her room that last evening, she never went back to her body. All ties there were long severed, and there was no reproach or regret for its failure. Instead she just gently kissed her parents as they held each other at her bedside.

Neither appeared to feel the touch. They were too intent on watching their daughter's life disappear with the bleep on the nearby screen.

Sarah walked through the door as the sound of her final heartbeat died.

Outside in the corridor, cuddled by an older woman whose hair was turning prematurely grey, was a young teenager. I had seen them before: Sarah's maternal grandmother and younger sister, Ruth.

Sarah's arms encircled them both for a brief hug, and while doing so she gently placed a soft kiss on each wet cheek.

At that moment Ruth reacted as though a light breeze had brushed her face: she instinctively reached up and touched the spot with her fingers. The small area was dry, as though blown by a warm breath.

I watched as Sarah grinned at her sister's response: a last sisterly tease!

In the past I have often wondered how we would look in the life after, once the physical body begins to fade. Well, in this "halfway house" world we look exactly the same, but somehow a more transparent version of ourselves. I don't mean to say that we are ghosts – only in the sense that all pretence and disguise are gone. You can literally see through into our souls. What you see if what you get – for good or ill.

That's how I now saw Sarah as she gave me her

parting smile – more warm than mere flesh and blood – and left me.

When I see her again – beyond the light – will she look the same, will I recognise her? Perhaps an heightened sixth sense will replace all other sensation. I cannot know, for only a very short while ago I could never have imagined the world I now inhabit.

So our original party became smaller- only Joan and James remained, and increasingly they were to be found huddled together – whispering – in some quiet corner.

I might, justly, have felt abandoned, or resentful, except I was too busy. I was certainly not lonely: In an hospital you can always guarantee a steady supply of new arrivals, and our spiritual waiting room was soon filling up again.

With Joan's focus on James, I found myself as a sort of reluctant mother superior – if only in deference to my age. Joan's withdrawal from public life also created another problem – it left a vacant post.

From now on all my future training would be "on the job." And so it began, and continued, until once again the approach of my favourite season: spring.

Without the gift of hindsight, or development of second sight, I did not realise how far this learning experience had taken me. That discovery came to me during one of my "in the body" moments: when I had more time for thought. There was precious little else to do – my body was functioning quite well without the control of an over critical brain. Too well, and often the lack of a censor between mind and mouth caused embarrassment to others, but the only one I cared about was Beth. It saddened me that I hurt her by my careless tongue.

There was very little I could do to help her: I could barely look after myself!

The once familiar body was slowly becoming "vacant:" It was as if every time I left it some malicious sneak thief crept in and removed more and more of my possessions. Oh all the usual contents remained: the flesh and blood which I had thought made "me." But something was slowly slipping away.

What it was I do not yet have the wisdom, or words, to describe. What little remained, was a terrible physical burden. But one I could put down. So, Beth forgive me, I took the easy way out and spent more and more time where I could be useful – the hospital.

One thing this weakness provided was plenty of practice, so by the spring, although I would never be perfect, I was becoming very good at my "job."

But I missed Joan – I missed my friend.

In the last few weeks I had barely seen her: just brief glimpses and always with James. Their behaviour had not remained a cause of envy for long, but I was intrigued, and bursting with questions. None of which I found the time or opportunity to ask.

Despite our physical separation I still felt that link between us, which had been stretched but never snapped. So, one evening in early June, when I found Joan waiting in our old familiar meeting place, I was pleased, but not really surprised.

We spent most of the evening together: revisiting all our old haunts while, in an odd reversal of roles,

I introduced her to new "waiters." But that was how it should be, that was always the plan. It was to be our last time together: as we walked Joan answered all my questions, including those concerning James. Although, as it turned out, she did keep one piece of information to herself!

Just before a new beautiful dawn broke James himself joined us and we shared a few brief moments before all Hell broke loose.

There had been a pile up on a nearby motorway and it was all hands to the pump. I never saw either Joan or James again.

I assumed James had retreated to his body so as to avoid the horror of violent death, while Joan was dealing with other casualties.

It wasn't until some time later, when I was satisfied there was no "lost soul" unaccounted for, I realised Joan had gone. She had last been seen near our well known corridor, and immediately I went to the morgue, where I found the human remains of my dear friend.

I was not unprepared, she had told me as much during our last conversation, but I was still shaken by the reality.

I felt all the normal human feelings of loss but no grief – I knew she was not there.

Later the hospital grapevine brought the news James had returned permanently to his body – he had been given that second chance. Of course I was genuinely glad for his sake, but I'll admit to less noble feelings. I would be spared the problem of dealing with the troubled lad, and I was going to be very busy!

In one death I lost my mentor, colleague and friend, but she left me with a huge inheritance.

I found myself spending more and more time away from my body, and Beth.

So it was with great relief I learnt of the intended visit of my daughter in the autumn.

My grand daughter was in safe hands, which eased my conscience and I gave myself permission to leave her – after all what could go wrong?

Obviously I had a lot to learn about human nature. It was to be an expensive and painful lesson since it involved my own flesh and blood.

JOAN

I hated leaving Betsy, but I had told her everything she needed to know. It was my time. I had done all I could, but there was one bit of unresolved business.

Some weeks ago James confided to me the source of his problem, and this had absolutely nothing to do with death. In fact his fears were very much on this side of the divide, and concerned someone we all knew well, or thought we did. The truth was much worse than any one of us guessed.

During the early days of his coma James had become aware of a dark presence, which always came at night and, unlike his other visitors, never spoke. He had the strongest impression that this creature wished him nothing but harm.

Eventually he began to realise that this ghoul was more than a visitor, incredibly it was a carer. The telltale uniform soon gave that away. The fact that this presence was female did nothing to lessen his night terrors.

In fact he had run foul of our friend, or should I say fiend – the night nurse.

Betsy was absolutely right in her first instinct – the nurse, I shall not dignify her with a name, was a bitch, but she was more than that – she was a sadistic bitch.

I remember she passed right through Betsy on our first meeting. What my friend felt I never knew, and never asked. Any insight into that dark soul was an experience I did not wish to share. Although at the time the nurse gave no obvious reaction to the contact I now wondered. It occurred to me our evil angel had steered well clear of Betsy ever since. Had the nurse felt something after all? Had she felt someone pass over her grave?

Once I learnt from James the details of his systematic abuse at her, not so caring, hands, I went with him to witness this for myself.

I never made the classic mistake of doubting the victim. I believed him completely. He was basically a good kid who had made a couple of bad decisions, but they were not irreversible.

He was more sinned against than sinning, and deserved another chance.

If our malignant Florence Nightingale had anything to do with it I don't think he would get that chance – that's how dangerous I feared this woman was.

James was right to be scared of leaving his helpless body alone with her – hence his reluctance to be with us.

Her career choice was a mistake, but not hers: she enjoyed all the power it gave and was setting herself up as judge, jury and, unless we could prevent it, executioner.

When I saw for myself the extent of her premeditated cruelty I was determined all my efforts would be diverted to solving this problem. For some reason she had taken against James, and he had become her special "project." All the most spiteful and humiliating treatments were reserved for him.

Yet it was even worse because this torment was carried out under the pretence of care – for his own good.

My hand itched to slap her smug face, but instead we bided our time, waited – and planned. But we needed a distraction if James was to survive and I was the one to provide it.

I had learnt enough over my time here to be able to exert some control over my hitherto lifeless body. Now I used that knowledge to make sure the nurse's night shift became as hectic as possible: shifting her venom to me and away from James.

As soon as her attention strayed back to the helpless young man at the other end of the intensive care ward I set up enough bodily disruption to bring her charging back to my monitor. Of course this, as intended, transferred much of her frustration to my poor helpless, old body, but I could take it. Besides, she would have been disappointed to learn, I couldn't feel anything – except the indignity of violation. Anyway it wouldn't be for much longer!

So we waited until my time was right and I had taught James all he needed to know.

It was my last evening. I met Betsy and we spent the night together: walking the wards and saying goodbye. Without any intention she was innocently showing me how well she could replace me, and I was satisfied. It was time to leave.

I do believe in the concept of free will, but I also believe in some higher force – call it what you will: God, Kismet, Fate, Destiny – your choice.

The next dawn an early dazzling sun blinded a lorry driver and caused him to swerve on a busy motorway. The resultant collision brought multiple casualties and chaos to our A & E. Remarkably there were no fatalities requiring our attention, but Betsy never discovered this until James and I had gone.

Our first destination was Intensive Care: quiet as most staff were in the overstretched emergency room. There was, however, one dark figure still at her post, or rather my bedside.

James went back to his body, – just in time to witness what we had planned, and our nurse had threatened. The previous night, in a rash moment of unchecked anger, she had promised to turn off my life support machine.

No doubt she had meticulously planned to get away with it. She had not planned the sudden revival of James, who was well briefed for this moment and immediately raised the cry for help. The alarm brought a nurse from her station, who had, fortuitously, booked in early for her day shift. She was astonished to see a nurse tampering with life preserving equipment.

An obviously skilled multitasker she unceremoniously pushed the offender out of the way while calling for security. She would make a very competent witness.

She was an excellent nurse, of that there was no doubt, but she couldn't save me. It was too late. No one would consider this a mercy killing, but for me that's exactly what it was. Ironically the nurse's final professional act had been one of kindness.

OK she had never intended it as such – but isn't that what irony means?

I had the satisfaction of staying long enough to see her led away in handcuffs.

I looked across at James. I knew he could no longer see me, but I saw him smile. It was the first time I had seen such an emotion on his face, and it was an incredible sight. A truly beautiful transformation.

As I lost sight of him behind a screen of bewildered nurses and doctors I said my goodbyes.

Everything would be all right now – I had no doubt whatsoever – James would be just fine.

God bless you, James, God bless you Betsy, my dear friends. I will see you again, but not yet.

Chapter Seven

May 1988

ELIZABETH

Its been a while since I picked up my diaries again, I knew what was coming. I knew it so well that there was no need to open and pick at that old decaying wound.

So I skipped one year completely, as I had many of the entries in it – some feelings are just too extreme to try to describe.

1987 was not a good year. It started badly and ended without improvement.

It really began I suppose a few months earlier in 1986, when I went away on a holiday which is no longer important enough to recall, except as the catalyst for future events. What happened was heartbreaking enough, but the real tragedy is that it should never have happened.

Certain events form milestones in our lives: they are all memorable for being either really good, or really bad. This milestone was about as bad as it could get. So bad I wish I could erase the writing on it, as easily as I pack up that unopened diary and hide it away again.

Well meaning people often give the advice to "forgive and forget," and I can understand all the reasons why that would be a good suggestion – not least for my own peace of mind. But when I ask the question, quite seriously, "how do I do that?" the honest answer is "I don't know." I have always valued honesty, but it is not an easy virtue and only one person has had the courage to give that reply.

I suppose, if I too am honest, one of the reasons I cannot reach a state of forgiveness is that I simply do not understand what happened the previous autumn. I desperately want to, but to do that I need to enter another person's state of mind.

My grandmother was so easy: we were like kindred spirits, or as Emily Bronte puts it so beautifully "whatever our souls are made of, hers and mine are the same." Words were always just a confirmation of what we already felt.

This was never the case with my mother: perhaps there was some initial bond. Old black and white photographs seem to show a genuine affection between a new mother and her baby – but the camera can lie, or at least mislead.

The sad truth is I will never know the reasons behind what took place when I went away in September 1986.

But I do know what happened – and it proved too much to comprehend.

Perhaps someone with a more generous nature, or stronger faith, could reach a state of forgiveness – but I have not arrived there…

The facts are that my mother, with the help and encouragement of a friend, took her unsuspecting mother on a couple of trips almost as soon as I left the house. It turned out neither were primarily for the purpose of shopping.

The first was only a short walk to our local bank. Where the manager was easily persuaded of my grandmother's mental competence, so easily that he transferred her bank book and money into my mother's name.

The second was longer: a twenty minute bus journey into the city, where an appointment had been pre arranged with the friend's solicitor to set up a new will.

All of this was bad enough but its method was what really hurt, because it was all done behind my back under the pretence of help. She would later explain when confronted by her angry, confused eldest child, that she was only protecting us. How could that be – did my grandmother need protecting from me, and did I need protection from myself. Even if this were true – what an insult to us both.

But it wasn't true: all those years she had quite happily left us to our own devices – what was different. Well I could only see two answers to that: a couple of thousand pounds in my grandmother's savings – and the house. It wasn't money, or even bricks and mortar to me, it was my birthplace – my home.

But the house, as she discovered: and she did search, was untouchable. I never thought I would have cause to be grateful to my local council – but such is the strange twist of fate.

Some years previously I had, thanks to a council grant and loan, had a new bathroom and kitchen extension built. At the time they had suggested it would be easier, for repayment purposes, if the house deeds were transferred into our joint names. I perhaps need to explain a little about the legal implications of this. Don't worry it won't take long!

A joint tenancy simply means that on the death of either owner the entire property reverts to the other. The alternative is a Tenancy in Common – which allows each owner to leave their half to whomever they like.

Of course a joint tenancy can be changed to a tenancy in common, and vice versa, but with one vital requirement: the other owner must be advised.

Therein lay the rub: my mother did not want me to know what she was doing, and this deception gave me a protection I didn't realise I needed.

At the moment I was blissfully ignorant of all this, in fact it was several moments – seven months in fact – before my eyes were opened.

I felt so stupid, although I knew my mother and I had never been close, I always had hope – like Pandora's box. Only when my box opened even that flew away and nothing was left.

The saddest thing is when I returned from my holiday in September 1986 I was more hopeful than ever for the future. My mother had been there when I needed her most – everything was going to be better – I was not alone. In reality I had never been so helpless. Would it have been better to remain in ignorance? I honestly don't know, but ignorance doesn't make it any less true, and I have always valued the truth.

It didn't really matter anyway, because as Gran reverted more and more to childlike behaviour, her capacity to think before she spoke became less and less.

Everyone knows that it is nigh impossible for a child to keep a secret: unless under extreme circumstances of threat or fear. Gran was restrained by neither. My mother, with two children of her own, would have been wise to remember that.

Gran and I never stopped loving each other dearly, but it would have taken a saint not to become frustrated with the situation. Gran was closer to this condition than I, but there were moments when even she was driven to hurtful verbal retaliation.

So many things became so difficult, and it must have been galling for her, a strong independent woman, to lose her dignity. It must have been hateful for her to find herself in such a dependant position, where each day little by little, she lost more and more control.

The smallest daily chores became a major battle, and in April 1987, following a particularly stressful bath time session, my grandmother's irritation revealed just a hint of what had transpired the previous autumn.

Not much, but enough for me to wonder, and worry.

So it began, the doubts and soul searching – which made my face age and my brain swim.

I know now it was a form of grief – a loss – and like grief I went through all the usual stages. They were easily recognisable because I had already been through them with my grandmother's illness.

This time the transition from denial, through anger, bargaining, depression and finally acceptance was a much swifter process. So much so that I never really left anger behind.

I didn't really have the luxury of time. I had to find out if I was going to be homeless when my usefulness was over. Harsh, but true When I think about it now I realise that was my worth – I wasn't even essential, but I was useful. It was a hard lesson to learn, but one never forgotten.

On the practical side I had to find out exact details. So in the middle of the emotional upheaval of Alzheimer's I felt myself dragged down further by the need to find out the extent of my mother's betrayal. Yes it's a strong word but that's how I felt, how I still feel.

I cannot come to terms with why she behaved so, or why I deserved it. She was a generous loving mother to my brother and sister: why could she not love me?

What had I done – was I so monstrous – she often said as much when I was a young child – but always out of my grandmother's earshot. All these negative little memories began to resurface and the implications staggered around my tired brain like an exhausted hamster on a wheel.

It was of course hopeless: I could no more hope to step into my mother's brain than I could a stranger's – and that was probably the most awful discovery. I had never known my own mother, or how much she must have disliked me.

As I grew up I always reasoned that any hardness towards me was as a surrogate to my absconding father. Up until then it never felt personal. Now it did.

When you are in so much emotional pain you do

what I did by the end of 1987 – you protect yourself. You put up barriers and numb your emotions. In short you learn to survive.

As time went on I came to some sort of resolution in the fact that I ended up pitying my mother. Pity is not a positive emotion, but its better than anger.

It was such a waste – for all of us. She could have had so much, and she threw it all away – for what? Some old festering resentment – I wanted to break the circle but not sure I have succeeded.

In all of this I never blamed my grandmother, but I did envy her loss of memory – she was spared all this wretched reality. There was no more certainty about anything – decades of dreams destroyed in just one week

Sometimes in my darkest moments – the small hours of the night, when buried thoughts have a habit of resurrection – I even wondered if Gran hated me too.

But in the clear light of day, when "the black dog of depression" fell asleep I know the other side of truth – the one that sets you free – she always loved me and always would.

PETER

I don't remember about why I am here – the last thing I remember was climbing a ladder. I even remember why – I was clearing an elderly neighbour's guttering.

But I don't think I ever got that far – I wish I had. I wish I had completed that at least.

Why do I think that?

God my head aches.

I think I should get up and find some aspirin.

Can't seem to raise myself out of this bed

Is it a bed – I try and turn my head to see – not a damn thing happens.

Perhaps it's a bog – that's it I'm in a bog – I must have fallen in

What the hell am I talking about – why would I be in a bog!!!.

Now I remember – I fell, but I don't remember landing – like one of those nightmares.

You say if you land you are dead – how would anyone know?

Think I went back to land of nod again – seems to be darker now than before.

I can't see me at all, and have major panic because my head wont move.

All those dreadful old tales come to mind about being paralysed.

Off again seems to be lighter – someone sitting beside me.

Older lady – is it the neighbour come to apologise please don't – I am so tired – just let me sleep.

I cannot move – I am so fucked (no don't say that – doesn't seem right here) no place for four letter words, or it is six!

Stupid here I am stuck in this bog and I'm sodding worried about bad language.

Shit, shit, shit – no stop it don't do that – someone may be listening – it feels as though someone is listening.

Are my eyes open – no – did I drift off again. I think I open them and see that the figure is still there.

Sitting down at the side of my bed – there a light shining down on me, but out of the corner of my left eye I see that she (it is a she) is in shadow.

I try really hard and manage to move my head slightly in her direction, but not sure if I really want to see her face.

What if she is ugly – I don't mean bad looking – no what if she is like that apparition in that recent film.

What if the sight of her drives me mad – oh great so now I'm going to be a nutter and paralysed (no don't even go there)

Falling, falling, falling – gone again.

Open my eyes and think "oh my God" (seem to mentioning him a lot now)

What about Hannah – my girlfriend – why did I just remember her?

Figure is still there – not Hannah – hands are old

– wrinkles and veins and those curious age spots – one reaches out and takes mine. I react – my hand gently squeezes hers – thank God (again) at least I can move my hands, and she's warm. Maybe not so bad – dare I hope.

And the headache has stopped – better and better. Send swift prayer – haven't done that since Sunday School.

Gone again but not long and I think something wakes me up this time – sounds like phone. Ringing, ringing – please shut up. Someone answer it PLEASE.

Now I want to get up and my visitor seems to understand because she leans forward into the light and I see her face.

Nothing to worry about – she is just an old woman – but she is really lovely.

Not a word I use so what do I mean?

I think I mean comforting – like a real granny – not the wolf in Red riding hood.

She speaks and her voice matches her face – it is soft, soothing and she asks.

Would you like to get up.

Of course I would and I get up – its so easy now – no more bog, no more pain.

She nods – and says it's too noisy here now lets get away from here.

I am aware of another figure pushing past me – seems to be in a rush.

I am strangely peaceful – normally I would be looking back – to what all the fuss is about.

But something is drawing me away and I follow the old lady (for I know she is a lady), although not like one of those stuck up titled women on the tv.

I must still be tired because I have job keeping up with her.

Why am I following a complete stranger – then I know.

Ahead of me I see Hannah waiting.

But this cannot be right – then I remember I fell off the ladder two years ago – I met Hannah in the hospital – she's a nurse!

But now she's not – at least she's not dressed like a nurse.

What IS she wearing?

I get closer and I see.

Is this some sick joke. Why would Hannah be wearing that in hospital?

Now for the second time this evening (I think its evening) someone puts out their hand to me and I take it. It's soft and warm and I grasp it like grim death.

Then it hits me – then I remember everything.

That party – the Halloween party – Hannah surprising me with her costume: and giving her wonderful contagious laugh. After all, she says, aren't nurses referred to as angels. Haven't I called her that myself. She's right and no one fits the role, or outfit, better.

I try not to remember – but it's all replaying in slow motion.

The journey to the party: I am driving Hannah's car. A Mini – strange the details you think are important – when they are not.

A wet dark evening

Suddenly something on the unlit country road, and Hannah, with that compassionate instinct I love so much in her, grabs the wheel and we swerve.

Stop this – don't go on, but Hannah is here, so it is all right.

So I carry on remembering when I should have stopped.

I feel the steering wheel shudder in my hands, and I lose control as the front wheels hit the boggy verge.

I think I shout, but no one listens – Hannah is too busy screaming – or is that sound just within my head.

For a few moments it is then all chaos: too much information flooding the senses.

Sight is blurred by motion, and touch confused in the melee of so much impact, but there is an overpowering scent of petrol, the sound of breaking metal and shattering glass.

A sudden bone wrenching jolt.

Then something else I recognise: the lingering unpleasant memories of a trip to the dentist- the distinctive taste of blood.Then it is over and all is silent and still.

I don't want to see anymore, so I squeeze my eyes tightly shut. Perhaps I can try and block the images or change them.

When I open them again Hannah still stands there holding my hand and smiling. And I know everything is OK.

I suddenly realise how ridiculous her angel costume should appear. But it does not – just wishful thinking – given we are both dead.

But that doesn't matter either – what matters is we are together and I suddenly know how it feels to be truly alive!

I have almost forgotten our companion, my guide, when Hannah turns to her and simply says, "thank you for bringing him back to me." Women, even in the afterlife it seems, are much better at this sort of thing. Few words are spoken, but volumes understood. The two just smile at each other before Hannah leads me onward, like a lost child found.

BETSY

Peter is gone now, but I remember him so well. I have a special reason to do so.

Like many lost souls, he was in denial. I remember him because at that time so was I.

I don't know how it happened, I thought it was so safe, even right, to abandon my body for that one week.

My grand daughter didn't need me – she had her mother. Besides she was going away: on a long overdue and deserved holiday. My daughter would take care of what remained of me.

Plus, it was busy at the hospital – but I cannot use that as an excuse – the only real excuse I have is naive trust. It is daft to think we can read another person's mind, even when we helped create it.

In my own right mind I would never have agreed to what I did that autumn.

The nearest similarity I can reach is sleep walking. I didn't remember a thing.

When I returned to my body it was like waking up and discovering with incredulity the stupid and possibly dangerous things you have done.

But how did I know – I wasn't actually there at the time – but somehow it stuck in my mind, like a bad dream, a very bad dream.

How did it happen – what happens when I am out of my body?

I quickly wrote off the possibility that someone, or thing, took up residency.

There had been no squatters. I don't have the defence of possession, demonic or otherwise.

Rather what remains is more easily manipulated by outside forces. Like a child being eager to please – especially those they love.

My body had been much the same as when I left it, except rather than something missing, there was something new. Something I must try to remember.

Mostly I can ignore fresh memories, in fact usually I have a problem recalling them at all, but now I knew it was important.

It took me until the new year to remember all the details, and until Easter to believe them.

I have let Beth down and I have to tell her. Not because I need to salve my own conscience. I have thought about it a long time, but I cannot convince myself this is a case of least said soonest mended.

Beth needs to know in order to protect herself, since, for the first time since she was placed in my arms all those years ago, I have failed her.

I feel so miserable, not just because I have to admit I am no longer capable of controlling myself – let alone helping her, but I am the cause of all this grief.

There was no question – I would much rather have died…

And there was another reason for my decision: we have always been totally honest with each other – except before I have always been there to help pick up the pieces…

She may even hate me, and I couldn't blame her if she did.

So in the spring of 1987, I took courage from the fresh, as yet spotless day, and told her in the only way I could.

It was not good.

I blurted out a few details more like an accusation than confession – almost like it was Beth's fault. Damn this stupid, stupid body – nothing comes out right any more. But it doesn't really matter about me – as long as I get through to her…

One look tells me I have. There's an horrible mixture of confusion, shock, and pain in her expression. Something I have never seen before.

I have never struck Beth in her life: there was no need, my voice was enough. But looking at her now I know exactly how she would have looked – like a slap in the face.

I have to leave – call me a coward, but I cannot bear to see her like this.

Before I go I risk one brief glance.

Not long, but enough to know that she doesn't hate me – she will never hate me and I don't know if I am sorry or glad.

I deserve some punishment: this remorse and misery is not enough.

Maybe I will find a way to reach Beth.

But for now I need to feel useful, I need to make amends, and if I cannot do it here I must go elsewhere. So I slink back to the hospital.

Chapter Eight

January 1989

BETSY

I went back to the hospital.

Since last year many people have passed through, slightly less have gone back.

I sometimes wonder how they think of their experiences now.

Do they risk talking about it, and face ridicule from our enlightened society, or do they keep their silence, and live in peace. Perhaps they are lucky in being able to convince themselves it was all a dream.

I cannot blame them if they choose the latter. They might find themselves out of one hospital and into another – more secure – establishment.

As a species we may have learnt to question, but we have lost the patience to wait for an answer. If we do we may not bother to listen, unless it suits the mind we have already made up.

Civilisation is not a place for the unfamiliar to be tolerated.

I often have the horrible conviction that if Jesus returned today, he would still be ridiculed, tortured and murdered.

Perhaps I am wrong: there are plenty of people I know who are not understood, but still respected. In fact shortly I was to meet one of these special individuals,

This may bring up a question – how do I know when I am needed? Oh you sceptics will probably joke that it involves some sort of spiritual bleeper. In fact that's not far from the truth.

I simply experience a call, which is neither heard, nor seen. But it is a feeling: like being tugged in a particular direction. Its that sixth sense again, but without experience, or at least an open mind, I cannot hope to explain it to you, so I won't waste both our time. Enough to say that it was one of these calls which drew me to Jenny. Jenny is a "guide" at a nearby hospice, and we crossed paths when one of my "charges" was transferred there.

This was not at all unusual: many terminal patients are moved to such specialist care homes. In fact Jenny had been one, and yes Jenny is dead in the mortal sense of the word. Yet she is most lively character I know in either world.

I should explain a little more here. The deceased have a choice – and sometimes they choose to stay. This is most common where the person is young and has no ties in the afterlife. If their premature deaths were caused by misuse of free will, in the case of accident or murder, then they may be confused and unsettled.

Jenny was the victim of a drunken driver and was killed just before her twenty first birthday – she has been a "guide" now for over twenty years, but she still looks twenty. She is happy, fulfilled, and not yet ready to move on.

Perhaps the time will come when her mother or father pass through and then she will go with them.

Until that time she is content to stay close to the world from which she was cut off by too little conscience and too many whiskeys.

On the face of it we are opposite ends of a lifetime: she wants to stay while I want to go, but we both have one last important job to do. We both need to find our replacements.

Some souls are like Jenny: they have reached a state of acceptance where there is no place for rage or retribution. Others stay for exactly the opposite reason: they cannot forget. They cannot move on.

Even when their bodies have gone, what remains continues to inhabit their old haunts. These are the lost souls which share the earth with us and we describe as "ghosts."

Although Jenny looks so young, she is not inexperienced. After all she has spent almost the length of her natural lifetime in this "job" and I would be a fool not to respect her opinion. I may be many things, including gullible when it comes to families, but I am not a fool.

So it was to her I unburdened my guilty conscience about Beth.

I was surprised, quite some achievement given my recent experiences, that she gave no reply, but instead asked a question. "Would you like to meet a friend of mine?"

My relationship with Joan had prepared me for what happened next. Without a word Jenny walked off down a corridor and I followed her. I did have a serious feeling of 'I've been here before!' It wasn't far and I am sure Jenny could have "thought" us there, but somehow it always seems bad manners to just appear in someone else's room, even if they can't see us.

It was night time and only a low light lit the bedroom we entered. A figure was stretched out on her back in an adult cot bed. Her head was slightly raised, but even so her breathing was laboured. Her eyes were open and she stared ahead at the hand made paper butterflies which decorated the wardrobe door. She either could not see us, or chose not to.She was obviously very ill: her skin colour was noticeably yellow, even in this poor artificial light, and there was something abnormal about the contrast between her skeletal arms and swollen body. With most people this would have been all they saw, all that mattered.

Every one of us are prone to make lasting judgements based on first impressions, but here was not the case. Apart from the initial shock, physical appearance meant nothing because all I saw was a very beautiful woman with a very extraordinary soul.

This was how I first met Susan, the most courageous, and modest, person I have ever known. Yes, you cynics will say, no one is perfect – of course you are right – but that's what makes us special. We can accomplish the most amazing things, despite our imperfections and temptations.

Susan did an amazing thing for me: in these final days of her life she taught me not only how to die with dignity, but also how to live without fear.

She was as trapped in her body as I was in mine, but she chose not to escape.

This is the story of Susan's end of days, as told to me by Jenny.

JENNY

I first met Susan when she came to the hospice following palliative treatment at home. It was a decision she had made with her husband some months earlier, when her condition was diagnosed as "terminal."

I say "met" Susan, but in fact we have never been introduced, formally or otherwise. Everything I know about her comes from observation. I don't know whether she sees me or not. If she does she chooses to ignore me, and I respect that.

She has lost too much independence already. I would not begrudge her this choice.It would be so easy for her to abscond, if only for a little while. The long lonely evenings and nights are the worst – they always are! So what would be so wrong with a little respite therapy? I don't know, because we do not talk.

Perhaps she is worried that if she lets go she will not want to return. Perhaps she wants to share all the happiness and, yes, misery of this world while she can.

She certainly isn't frightened of death, or unsure of the future. She has a faith which puts us all to shame, and that includes the church minister who tries to bring a certainty without conviction.

It is not death, just its manner, which concerns her. She does not want to pass in pain, and she doesn't want her husband to see this.

Thanks to the wonders of modern medicine, and morphine, she is in no physical pain, but there is no remedy for emotional and mental distress – except perhaps distraction.

When Susan came to us she was already confined to a wheelchair and incapable of unaided movement below the waist. She cannot move without the help of two nurses and a hoist. She cannot even perform basic bodily functions unaided. But every morning, despite the indignity and discomfort, she is washed, dressed, and down in the day room by 10 am.

There she has returned to her love of art. With the help of a small desktop easel she produces the most painstaking creations: including the paper butterflies in her room.

Butterflies are a personal favourite: a symbol of rebirth – everlasting life.

The paintings are especially bright and colourful: full of life – fluttering butterflies and blooming flowers – often forget me nots. There isn't a visitor, or carer, who is not the proud owner of one of her works.

I had the feeling this activity is not solely to pass the time, or leave some sort of legacy, but because she is still very much alive.

Susan is a fighter, but she is not burying her head in the sand. She has faced the truth a very long time now, almost two years.

Since first diagnosis she has under gone every sort of medical treatment available, including two bouts of chemotherapy and two major operations. At first the outlook was good. In fact at the end of that first horrendous year she was given the all clear.

It was a wonderful Christmas present, but it was snatched away before Easter.

At the beginning of March last year a check up revealed the cancer had not only reoccurred but spread.

Yet Susan considers herself lucky.

She bases this on the fact that as a three month old baby she developed pneumonia and almost died. Everything since she views as a bonus.

So while this vicious disease may slowly be destroying her body, it will never take her spirit. It will never win.

Susan will not be remembered by anyone at the hospice with pity or embarrassment, just with much affection and great respect.

When people think of Susan they will recall her life, and not her death.

She is the life and soul of the place. She is younger than many – having just celebrated her sixty third birthday. But she does not complain about the unfairness of this any more than she sees irony in the fact she has never smoked yet is dying of lung cancer.

Night time I know is the most difficult time for her, as it is for all human life which depends on the beat of heart and breath of lungs. It is when all the demons and doubts arise – when you are truly alone with your own mortality.

Of course Susan could escape via her dreams, but she chooses to stay firmly in this world while she can.

She does so now, and focuses on her butterflies, placed there for tough moments like this – a symbol of hope.

So Jenny is silent and for a few moments we stand still in shared respect.

Susan's eyes eventually close and she falls into sleep, but not into dreams, at least not the ones which include us and our world.

Why I wonder does she do this, when it is so easy to avoid all this misery.

Later I see the answer for myself when her husband makes his daily visit.

Yes of course there is love, but there is something much more important – they actually like each other. This is the best sort of marriage – the sort I had with George. A partner who is also your best friend.

I remember that this is a wonderful, unique blessing, but it is double edged.

It gives mutual support, but it carries a great responsibility.

Colin, her husband, is desperately trying to be strong for her, and he knows what she needs will be torture for him. She needs honesty, she needs to be able to open up and he sacrifices his own feelings for her. That's what you do for someone you truly LOVE.

And then it strikes me – Beth – isn't that what we also have with each other. I have let her down, and I am not referring to the incident with her mother. I have been selfish. I have been so engrossed by this new life I forgot Beth is dealing with a different reality.

I have made the common mistake: I have looked after others while neglecting the person dearest to me on this earth. And for the moment I am still on the same tiny vulnerable planet…

Then it comes to me, Susan has not made that mistake. She is still alive and she is not shirking its responsibility. Sometimes it is pure joy, more often than not recently, it has been a great load, but one she will not put down.

Jenny understands: that's why she knew meeting Susan would be the best answer to my predicament.

While she has tried to help Susan, she has the wisdom to know when to leave matters alone. Susan has chosen to stay in her failing body as long as possible. She knows she will soon have an eternity. Time is only precious in this life, and she doesn't want to waste a second of it.

During the last week I have spent all my spare time at the hospice and it is only in the last couple of days, when Susan is almost comatose, that she asks for help.

But it is not help from Jenny, and it is not to live – it is to die. Of course no one can – Susan would never ask in her right mind because she knows the compassion of the law does not extend to her, or anyone assisting her.

It is hard for everyone – thankfully her parents were spared: they died the year before her initial diagnosis, but it is not for long.

I am humbled by her spiritual strength, but her body is very, very tired and on that final day I watch as she slowly slips away. We, on both sides of the divide, are praying that her ordeal will soon be over. At last we are answered and at 10.30 pm she whispers her last words to Colin "I love you."

Such suffering might be enough to make you doubt your own faith, but Susan's is so strong that it is infectious. She leaves us all wiser – and sadder.

Neither death nor disease can claim any victory – Susan won after all.

The cancer will die with her body but she will carry on.

There is always a plan, and there is always a choice, but sometimes the plan is the best choice. This was the case with Jenny and Susan.

Jenny planned well, and she has found her replacement. Susan was a perfect choice – she will be strong but sympathetic.

I have the feeling, though, that she will continue here for a long time, at least I hope it will be long, her husband's lifetime. Life is not everything, but it is irreplaceable and therefore precious. Susan knew that, and she taught it to me.

So now I have to leave – time to put what she taught me into action.

It was time I went back – back to Beth.

Another lesson I learnt from Susan, is the importance of human warmth, something I realise I have missed.

All I want to do now is hug Beth.

Chapter Nine

March 1989

ELIZABETH

It's been a long, difficult – and busy time. My grandmother's mind has deteriorated to the point that all of her memories are in the long past, and her present centres around "what time is it?"

On the other hand her body compensates for the inactivity of the brain, but this is not a bonus. The closest I can come to it is like dealing with a head strong, and very large toddler, who is into everything.

But while young children are exploring a new world, I sometimes feel Gran is clinging on to hers.

Whatever the reason in practice it means I spend less time working and more time supervising my "charge." My freelance work has been cut, and my free time non existent. Fortunately this combination at least means that I have little need for pocket money, Between my part time work, and Gran's pension, the bills are paid.

Perhaps this should have made me resentful, but the miracle is, it did not.

Maybe I have come to terms with my mother's interference – or perhaps I am just exhausted.

I have learnt one thing: when you are being

stretched to your limits on a rack, you barely notice your finger nails being pulled out.

That's how it was the first year after my enlightenment – the only way I can dispassionately describe what happened with my mother.

There was information I needed to know, and jobs I had to do, in order to relieve my worries about the future, but once they were done I just carried on.

It is amazing just how much you can bear when the weights are added slowly over time. Little by little my load increased, a pressure which should have crushed me, but somehow I kept dragging on.

Had I come to terms with my mother, well in a way, yes. Although I still cannot forgive the action, I can accept that my mother is neither me, nor my grandmother, and be everlastingly grateful for that fact.

It is now spring, 1989, and this diary shows me how tired and overwhelmed I have become. Nothing distinguishes one day from another – I now know where the expression "daily grind" comes from!

But I turn a page and suddenly everything changes – I remember.

The entry is simple, but it recalls so much more than I have written. It brings back the fresh scent of spring – replacing the dead smell of rotting leaves and cold soil. The aroma of hope!

I remember I had been out in our long garden. Perhaps I had briefly escaped the claustrophobia of the four walls I loved, or, maybe I was walking down my own memory lane. Revisiting the past in the awakening flowers and shrubs that my grandmother had established and nurtured over the decades of her life.

So how have we got on – well that too is acceptance – and once more a well loved and much quoted prayer comes to mind: "God give me grace to accept with serenity the things that cannot be changed."

When I returned from the garden I was in for a surprise – rather than the usual shock, I found my grandmother standing in the kitchen. I thought at first she was putting the electric kettle on the electric plate, a common, and potentially dangerous, mistake, but no: she was looking at me.

Actually looking at me, and there was a light in her eyes I hadn't seen for ages. There was someone at home, and through those illuminated windows there was a soul.

Although in all her worsening decline I can honestly say Gran never failed to recognise me – I never had to face that particular heartbreak.

She came towards me and gently put her arms around me. She held me and simply said, "I do love you you know." In that second all the old warmth flooded back as strongly and comforting as the scent of her talcum powder. I sank into a familiar, almost forgotten embrace and replied, "I love you too,"

It felt an inadequate response, but sometimes words are not enough.

For a few moments, which felt like a lifetime, we just stood in that small kitchen hugging each other and crying.

They were not tears of frustration or sadness, but joy, and I was reluctant to let go. I was not under the illusion life would be different, or Gran would be "cured." I just wanted to store this moment to recall in the difficult times I knew were ahead.

I was right, this was almost the last time we bridged that widening gap, but after this day the dreams began.

They were amazing dreams – in them my grandmother came back to me as she used to be. Not every night, but those when I felt at my lowest ebb.

The strange thing was as she became less herself – less there, the dreams became more real and more frequent.

When I was young she always used to cuddle me and say "everything is going to be all right." In fact it was a well known family joke that she was something of a witch. My most precious dreams were those where she held me and whispered the well-known prediction. I always believed her then and I believed her now. Somehow everything was going to be OK. Oddly enough, despite all this nocturnal activity, I slept well. The only down side was my reluctance to leave my grandmother and wake up But, when I did, I always felt recharged and even optimistic for the coming day.

It might only be a dream, but it was beautiful and so real – more real than my daily nightmares.

Whatever it was I didn't analyse it too deeply – it was my lifeline, and I clung to it for all I was worth.

BETSY

I went back to Beth the next morning after Susan's death. I had spent the hours between thinking. Something I had deliberately tried to avoid since letting her down so badly.

I had come to no decision regarding how to help Beth, but I would start with my first instinct, I just wanted to hold her again: to feel her human warmth.

I was sick of my sixth sense. At the moment it was useless to Beth – I needed to exercise the other five.

When I returned it was to our living room, and it was empty. In those first private moments I had more time for misgiving.

What if Beth rejected me – I couldn't really blame her. God only knew to what depths my mind and body had sunk. Yes, I had been back occasionally – just flying visits. Enough to know that my body was still at home and not in hospital or nursing home.

So Beth had kept me with her – I am not sure if I felt better or worse about that. I thought I deserved some punishment, and Beth deserved a break, but I confess to being secretly glad we were still together.

In these brief visits I found Beth distracted, and sometimes short tempered.

As if she had no energy to spare for emotion. I hoped and prayed there would be some affection left for me.

Next my concern went to more practical issues – would my body respond to control – or had I left it too long.

Like most anticipated difficulties, time magnifies the problem and the fear: it was, in fact, much easier than I thought.

My flesh was weak and my spirit was not only willing, but very determined. Besides suddenly I had no time for further thought.

I heard a deep sigh, and Beth's slow footsteps approaching from the garden.

I quickly put my brain into gear and used the old telegram system to send messages to my body. It worked – I suppose its like riding a bike – although I never managed to master that in my lifetime.

My legs worked and took me up the step into the kitchen, where I stopped trying to focus through my old, inadequate eyes. It was like looking through very dirty, scratched, spectacles.

Beth stopped in the back door, obviously preparing herself for trouble.

During this pause she glanced around, probably to assess the situation, and finding nothing obviously wrong, turned to me.

I used all the strength I had, including that extra sense, to mentally reach out and let her know I was there.

Thank God I saw recognition and something more – if I could dare to believe it.

It gave me the courage to step forward, stretch out my arms and take her into them.

My words were murmured, partially through lack of practice, but mainly long overdue emotion.

It didn't matter, Beth responded, and cocooned together away from the present and its problems, we both slipped back into the past. We just clung to each other, cried, and for a brief while that's all there was. For a moment we were the only two people in the world. We had returned to a time when a cuddle with my grandchild was everything I needed.

But although it seemed timeless, it was over too quickly.

Neither of us wanted to let go, but we understood reality, and grudgingly released each other.

It would be enough for a while, but I knew Beth needed more. She needed help and how could I do that?

This effort had been exhausting, and I realised my body was no longer mine to control. As time went on it would be increasingly less and less so.

There had to be another way.

I determined that until I had an answer I would restrict my dreams to the night time.

Then it came to me – like a bolt from the blue. Or rather inspiration from above. Go back to where it all began.

If Beth couldn't follow me, then I would go to her. And the way – staring me in the face – my dreams, maybe I could reach her through them.

So it began.

Every night, I left my body and sat by Beth's bedside until she fell asleep.

This process usually didn't take very long, because she was so exhausted.

As soon as I heard her breathing slow and deepen into a snore, I began talking to her.

It was like going back to her childhood, to those bedtime stories I told her as she fell asleep. She never asked for books, not because she didn't like reading. In fact during the day she was a real book worm. Its just at night she preferred one of my unique made up fairy tales.

These new stories still began and ended with a goodnight kiss, but the content was a combination of past memories and future plans. It had the comfort of a verbal hug, and I know it did both of us good.

After a while her breathing would change again, and a smile appeared on her lips. Once I knew she was settled and at peace I left for my night shift at the hospital.

Chapter Ten

October 1990

ELIZABETH

According to my diaries, its been not a great year, but its been better than its predecessors.

Gran is obviously not improving, but somehow we carry on. We sometimes raise a smile and even manage the odd laugh.

A good rest is wonderful medicine and that's what I was getting – thanks to my nightly ration of dreams.

I don't remember dreaming so much before, and never, to my knowledge, so regularly, but I wasn't complaining. Some nights were filled with memories from the past, others fantasies about the future. An area I had not dared explore for some time.

Often the dreams were a combination of the two – past and future.

But they always had two things in common: they were filled with happy thoughts, and they all included my grandmother.

Every morning I would wake up refreshed, as though I had actually slept (another feeling I had not had in a long time). Even better the remembrance of my nights helped me to cope with the days of my present.

So I was not only coping, I was living. OK it wasn't a fantastic existence, but it was better than the previous few years. Also I discovered something truly important – I wasn't alone.

Suddenly it seemed I had acquired a small, but devoted, group of supporters, and in such circumstances quality is certainly better than quantity.

You find out who your real friends are, and one of them was also a neighbour, Alice. We shared much, including age and a relationship with Alzheimer's. Her father, and therefore her family, had suffered from its effect some years earlier. He was now dead, but the memory lingered on.

We shared something else, something precious, a strong sense of humour.

The best antidote for misery is laughter – even if it is directed at yourself. Of course some of my grandmother's antics were the trigger for this entertainment, but she was never the target. We didn't mock her, rather the situation. And, I like to think, she would have been the first person to enjoy the joke.

Alice was another lifeline.

Every day, with Gran safely asleep in an afternoon nap, I slipped next door for a few moments therapeutic conversation. First I had to ensure that all necessary precautions were taken, which included turning off the oven and double locking the front door.

Then, over a relaxing cup of tea and homemade cakes, I used this time as an emotional socket to recharge. My neighbour's kitchen became my bolt hole: much more effective and much less harmful than valium.

Sometimes it was a case of mutual moans, sometimes humorous anecdotes, more often than not a combination of the two. It was a rare, and particularly bad day, which couldn't include some laughter. Thanks to Alice there were not many of those!

One series of incidents involved her and was a cause for such uncontrolled hilarity we hurt from stitch, and it wasn't just too much tea that necessitated a sudden rush to the bathroom.

The source of this amusement was my grandmother's unexpected interest in athletics, in the form of the shot putt. Of course Gran, thankfully, for my neighbour's welfare, had no such equipment, but was happy to improvise with the only suitable substitute available -Wellingtons.

There was quite a collection in our garden shed, or, should I say, had been quite a collection, most of them now littered Alice's garden. They were collected once a day and returned, with the wisdom it was better the missile you knew.

Wellingtons are not the most accurate of projectiles, but they are considerably softer than most other items found in the great outdoors.

For some reason, only known to Gran and never divulged to another living soul, Alice's garden was the target area for these objects.

It was a bizarre occupation, but it was not malicious. It kept her occupied, and gave us a laugh.

With the very young and very old you are sure of only one thing – you can never be certain of anything. Perhaps not quite accurate, since you are guaranteed to be regularly embarrassed.

With children there can be a sort of innocent charm to soften any humiliation, with the elderly no such consolation.

The next source of humour concerned this fact, while providing Alice and I with many hours of pleasurable chatter.

I need to explain that my grandmother was somewhat of a singer – although not a melodious one. Our family, I feel fairly sure, will never produce any records, unless for the worst karaoke rendition – ever!

Nevertheless in my childhood I heard all the old favourites from my grandmother's youth. Mainly these songs were old Victorian ballads – which in terms of depressing lyrics – would put American Country and Western narratives of doom and gloom to shame.

Most of them concerned death: young people dying for love; the middle aged dying for unrequited love; the elderly dying without love. Their writers, and audiences, were certainly not alarmed by strong subjects: accident, teenage suicide and domestic murder were all regular features. Some were far too poignant for me, and one in particular I found very disturbing.

Nowadays its Victorian sentimentality would be a cause for mockery. I can already hear your sniggers at its title "Don't go down the mine, Dad."

But before you do so, remember that pit disasters were a very real horror in 1910 when this ballad was written. In fact up until that date over 6,000 miners had been killed in accidents in Welsh mines alone. And that doesn't take into account the thousands more who died from respiratory diseases like "black lung."

So for my grandmother's generation there was genuine tragedy in the words she learnt. To give you some parallel, it would now be like ridiculing a song about famine, or genocide. While we cynical 21st century critics may poke fun at the maudlin nature of presentation we should be careful not to transfer this to its subject.

Many years later when repeated to me, my grandmother did it so earnestly that there was no place for laughter, not even the nervous kind. I always remember its second verse:

> *Don't go down the mine Dad,*
> *Dreams very often come true*
> *Daddy, you know it would break my heart*
> *If anything happened to you*
> *Just go and tell my dream to your mates*
> *And as true as the stars that shine*
> *Something is going to happen today*
> *Dear Daddy, don't go down the mine!*

Three years later in 1913 a colliery explosion in Senghenydd, South Wales killed 439 miners and 1 rescuer, the youngest casualties being just fourteen years old.

So what musical delights were our visitors treated to – or terrified by?

Well I can tell you one thing, all the death and love disappeared and from somewhere in the dark recesses of her memory very different songs surfaced. These are probably best described as "dirty ditties" – the verbal equivalent of the saucy seaside postcards.

I used to wonder where these came from, but now I rather suspect I know.

During the First World War troops from the local barracks were billeted in the house Gran shared with her own grandmother. I am sure the soldiers found great amusement in reciting their alternative war poetry to their hosts – which probably happened to include the keen ears of a fascinated young girl.

No one would blame the men. They were actually only boys themselves – soon to be facing the horror of some muddy foreign field.

One of the more repeatable verses never to be included in volumes on Great War poetry went as follows:-

I wish I were a diamond ring upon my lover's hand

Then every time she wiped her arse I'd see my promised land.

Eat your heart out Robert Graves!!

But there was a bizarre link to accepted military tradition, because it was sung to the regimental march of the 7th Calvary (Gary Owen). Not sure this was a tribute or insult. I suppose it could have been worse: many satires of that era were based on well known hymn tunes.

Maybe this was simply because they were the melodies the soldiers knew best, or possibly there was a more subtle motive. Never underestimate the intelligence of the so called "common" people. By lampooning the religious and military were they sticking two fingers up at the Establishment?

If so my great great grandmother would have approved. While she did not normally tolerate lewd language, she disapproved of organised mass murder more.

One problem solved, there was another question -- why was it these ditties were performed at the most sensitive moments – usually visits from the doctor, nurse or any other official representative. Maybe my normally demure grandmother was raising her own two digits to authority!

To be honest though, as time went on, my tolerance grew, and towards the end I didn't really give a damn. Politeness was way down on the list of my priorities!

Fortunately while my grandmother's language occasionally became a little suspect she never relapsed into that childlike behaviour which I like to refer to as "the flasher" syndrome.

Many people suffering from mental illness lose their inhibitions and often their clothes follow suit. This sort of striptease can range from forgetting single articles of clothing to literally naked exhibitionism.

Without seeming sexist I have to say, in my experience, the occasional lapse of dressing etiquette is a female trait: the sporadic forgetfulness of bra or stockings. On the other hand full exposure is inevitably a male preserve – hence the term "flasher." Why is it some men seem to consider the display of their dubious attributes a cause for pride rather than mirth? And why it is always those who obviously need stronger spectacles – or a magnifying glass!

Enough of this vulgar reflection, but it does give you an idea why Alice and I were such kindred spirits. Many times have we sat in such lofty discussion and laughed until our sides ached.

Luckily Gran had an attachment to her underwear which meant we, and any other visitors, were spared that embarrassment. In any case her panties were the bloomer variety, the kind resembling my old gym knickers – which you could stretch down to your ankles. Alice and I used to attend the same secondary school, so we could console each other about the indignity of wearing these "passion killers."Ironically, in my grandmother's case, these large baggy directoires protected her dwindling dignity. So if sometimes her seated position was a little less modest, or her skirts hitched up a little too high – it didn't matter. Her knickers covered a multitude of sins and usually her knees too!

On the whole I suffered minimal embarrassment from Gran's illness – if you discount the songs! Counting my blessings – I got off lightly.

Unlike my friend, I never had to worry about inviting a guest into the house with the dread that a naked geriatric waited to greet us.

BETSY

Jenny and Susan were busy: I confess to a little bit of envy – they have each other and I still missed Joan. But good luck to them. Jenny had been alone for a long time, and she deserved her good fortune in finding Susan.

I was too busy to feel jealous for long – the waiting room was almost full and there was a continual stream of people passing through.

For some reason though we "waiters" still met up in the morgue, and I never knew why. Except human nature is always the same regardless of circumstance, and it might just be a case of natural curiosity.

Margaret, my daughter, used to have a cleaning job in a funeral home, and would check newcomers to see if she recognised them. No small feat in itself because American cosmetic work is more extensive, and it doesn't matter if you are dead or not. Therefore, by the time the hairdresser and make up artist had finished with them, the laid back customer was often a caricature of their former self.

Could it be my "waiters" were not just checking for friends and family, but had a more personal interest in the corpse. This thought obviously hurt my feelings, because it implied some neglect on my part. But I have to say that during my shift no one ever found out about their passing from a toe tag. People are individuals whatever their situation: a combination of the best and worst of human nature.

Everyone is special, but some are more special than others, and it was near Christmas when I came across a real character, who went by the name of Gladys.

My usual nightly routine was checking for fresh customers, although, as I said before, I usually get a tug if anyone needs help. After this I deal with new "waiters" and take them to the meeting place (the morgue).

I was alone this evening, and everyone was preoccupied – checking bodies.

But not quite everyone – there was a stranger among us – someone I had not picked up from my ward round.

It was Gladys, she introduced herself and explained that she had come to us from an old peoples home, and was currently bobbing in and out of her body following a severe heart attack. This was not her first "out of body" experience in this hospital and she knew the ropes.

She was without doubt the most senior of us, and was more fed up with this life than she was frightened by the next. Her only complaint about 'popping her clogs', her expression not mine, was disappointment. She had expected to receive her telegram from the Queen next month, but now it looked increasingly unlikely. She was understandably miffed that she had lived for ninety nine years and would be deprived of her recognition by just a few weeks.

By her own accounts it had been a full life.

She reminded me so much of my own grandmother – who had brought me up. They were both generous with whatever they had. Often, in those days this was not money, but something much more valuable – their time. I remember those long, gas lit, evenings of my childhood were filled by our own entertainment. Most of it coming from my grandmother. Comical stories from her past, which made us all laugh, however many times we had heard them. Then, as night crept in, curtains were drawn and talk turned to tales of ghouls and ghosties. The fact that these were sworn as the absolute truth just added to the pleasurable tingle up the spine and shiver around the shoulders. Little did we know then just how real these stories were!

Usually the evening ended with a sing along. In our family not the most pleasant experience on the ear drums, and we had no musical instrument to drown the voices!

It was later the first evening when I heard Gladys singing one of the same old Victorian ballads which I learnt as a child.

Like my grandmother Gladys loved people, but when she came across a "wrong un" her sympathy was all with their victim. She had precious little patience with any arguments for tolerance.

She told me once that free will was a marvellous thing, but an awful responsibility and one you cannot shirk. It's no good blaming someone else, not even God, when you make the wrong choice. You have to live with your decision, especially when someone else dies because of it.

She was a person after my own heart and the first "waiter" I had met who I would have considered as my successor.

But, as I came to know Gladys better, I knew this was impossible. She often talked fondly about friends and family, all of whom had passed on. So I didn't ask because she might well say "yes." After waiting so long it would be selfish of me to delay their reunion a moment longer.

Besides I am a great believer in fate – somewhere out there was my perfect replacement.

For the time being though Gladys was a welcome addition to our fleeting little group and every night entertained us with stories of her life. It had been a long and eventful one, and she appeared to remember everything.

We listened to tales of her country childhood on a family farm, were gripped by her exploits in the Great War, where she served as a nurse in Flanders.

I couldn't help wondering if she had come across any of the young men who had left our home for the front line. I always suspected very few returned, and those who did were not the same people who left.

There was no point in asking – I never remembered their names. Sadly I imagine many of them are still unnamed: lying in a foreign field under the epitaph "A soldier of the Great War." Over the years, on every Remembrance Sunday, I have wondered about the body which lies in Westminster Abbey – could he have been "one of ours." Another Unknown Soldier.

Maybe I will soon know!

These conversations with Gladys were like those evenings spent with my grandmother. I love reading, but romantic fiction: almost like novel versions of the old ballads. When comes to the past I prefer a more old fashioned approach. I like to sit down and listen. There is a strange comfort in this which goes back centuries.

Before printed books, and the Puritan stress on everyone being able to read, people used to sit around the flickering light of an open fire and pass on their family histories by word of mouth.

Don't get me wrong I completely agree with equality of learning, and am forever grateful to that much maligned religious group for their liberal views on the education of the women.

In fact I have a very simple philosophy about this. There are three things which should not depend on the size of your purse, or shape of your body: education, health and justice.

It's just there should be room for all types of schooling. In this, less than perfect, world, a good education is often measured by wealth. So we "common" people need all the help we can get, and if that provides a few moments of light relief so much the better!

Gladys was certainly very good at this. A century of history brought to life with her words: seen through her eyes as one of us.

Every night we gathered together: the older people, like myself, to share memories. The younger audience would be fascinated by events they had previously only read about in school books.

I hoped that when, or if, they returned to their bodies they would discover a whole new respect and interest in their own grandparents. I knew both sides would benefit: so much previously wasted experience and wisdom.

But these yarns were not always about the past, some were about the present, and these were all related to Gladys' retirement home.

Most were not fit for a mixed gender and age audience. They involved the tendency of the elderly, as well as the young, to abandon their inhibitions.

Apparently the home had a very liberal attitude because the night time routine often found some interesting bed fellows!! As long as no one complained then they gave them the benefit of being consenting adults, and turned a blind eye.

After all the chances of an unwanted pregnancy were so remote as to be a miracle.

Gladys was not interested in this vice, but she enjoyed a sneaky midnight game of poker with several like minded friends, and a glass of brandy, or two.

And if some extra pension money was made at the same time, so much the better. The police were hardly likely to raid an old people's home for illegal gambling. Like most of our civilised society the authorities consider us as a nuisance – not as criminals, but by living too long! We seem to have become the scapegoats for every problem – governments always need a distraction for their own failings. In Roman times it was the Christians – so we are in good company.

Some of our younger members were quite shocked at such behaviour from geriatrics they considered "past it." Others were delighted by the refreshing revelation that, contrary to popular belief, there is life – and sex – after retirement.

Gladys had never married, never had children,

and could be thought a figure for pity, except those who really knew her could only feel envy. Hers was a life well and fully lived.

After the Great War she became a fierce supporter of women's rights.

Females were given the vote in 1918, but only if they were over 30 and held a professional or university qualification. It wasn't until 1928 when they received full equality with 21 year old males. There was much to change in the law – there still is in human attitudes.

One of the main problems was financial freedom. There were jobs for the 'weaker sex', but they were generally physically hard, usually extremely mucky and the lowest paid. Added to which married women were not expected to work – except in the unpaid drudgery of their husband's home.

Gladys was lucky having an inheritance. A rare gift since most family bequests went to the eldest male. In fact only a few years before Gladys was born married women were not allowed to leave a will. Not that this mattered since marriage transferred all their assets to their husbands, so they owned nothing to leave.

Gladys never took her good fortune for granted. It was not a vast sum, but it made her independent, and she made the most of it.

By the 1930s she was in her forties. But the great depression did not affect her spirits, except to make them stronger. She took up the cause for the unemployed, and supported the Jarrow Marchers – cheering them on their way as they passed her home.

She explained "home" was a vague description

because she spent a lot of time travelling, but that came to a halt towards the end of the decade. A little inconvenience known as the Second World War!

This minor event did not deter Gladys for long. She still had her parents' farm and was delighted to welcome a group of land army girls – whose exploits with the local lads provided us with two solid evenings entertainment.

Later in the war she left the farm in the capable hands of her marvellous regiment of women and moved to London. While people were evacuating London she took up residence in its heart.

Gladys, we knew by then, would never "blow her own trumpet," but reading between the lines we could imagine just what a great difference she made to her neighbourhood. Not just in terms of her sunny nature either.

In her fifties – halfway through her life – she was literally up to her neck in the rubble of bombed out buildings searching for the living or the dead. Any homeless were sure of food and shelter, and that included the four legged variety.

She described once how she had yanked a small bedraggled mongrel from the remains of a local house. He was the only survivor from the family, but he fell on his paws. He had not only escaped the organised slaughter which befell so many pets at the start of the war, but now he had been rescued a second time. He eventually found himself transferred to the country, where he earned his living culling the farm vermin and being spoilt by the land girls.

Rats – as he, not very originally, came to be known – survived the war and lived on into a new decade, but there was no peace just a different kind of conflict.

So in her late sixties, when most of her friends were enjoying a much earned retirement, Gladys had joined C.N.D., and was busy "banning the bomb."

Gladys life was like an illustrated history, but when we closed the book one evening it was never opened again. Perhaps one day it will be.

Chapter Eleven

March 1991

ELIZABETH

Another year, another diary – not many left now. In fact there is just one more completed book waiting on my bookshelf.

But, for now, back to my 1991 Dairy diary, bought from the milk delivery man. Each page is decorated with pictures of mouth watering food and accompanied by recipes, the results of which never seem to match these images.

Like the, less than perfect, reality of these meals, my words are lacking any interest.

Reading through them every day is very like its neighbours: the yesterday which is gone, the tomorrow which has yet to be.

But one spring day was different. As I read my entry I remember it now as if it were indeed yesterday: for all the wrong reasons. It was memorable because it was so shocking, and too close to home.

Horror you expect to be confined to a cinema or tv screen, or within the covers of a book. You do not expect to learn about it from the pages of your local newspaper.

For Alice and I it became THE topic of conversation, replacing all others. It was impossible to discuss anything else or change the subject to lighten the mood.

Murder is seldom a cause for humour, except perhaps the black sort depicted in literature or film. This was different. The killer was a sadist, and the victim was not only legally still a child, but beneath the age of consent. It made us feel uncomfortable because it made us question our own beliefs.

We all like to think we are civilised, and it is sobering to realise just how easily our primitive instinct can reassert itself.

Then you have to admit that it is not justice, protecting the innocent, or any other noble motive which drives your emotions – but good old fashioned revenge – an eye for an eye.

Neither Alice, nor I, are pro the death penalty, but without much consideration we agreed we would happily pull the switch on this monster, or, take a rusty knife to his genitals!

The appalling thing is we really meant it.

There are some crimes which are unforgivable, mainly because they are unbelievably wicked.

Any brutality involving children is just such an offence Psychiatrists may try to provide a defence. For us there was none possible – we all have a choice.

Anyone who chooses to hurt and kill a child is beyond the pale, beyond the compassion they denied to their victim.

To call such a creature an animal is an insult. Most other species defend their young with their own lives – only humans it seems regard them as fair game for self satisfaction, abuse and murder.

The details described in the newspapers went

through the whole gambit of journalism, from informative to sensational, depending on the ethics, or not, of their owners.

The unembroidered facts were bad enough, and made me ashamed to belong to the human race. A society which gave this monster the notoriety he craved, while forgetting – or even judging his victims – was not one I understood.

Although certain events are written down nowhere I remember them so vividly.

One was my return home later that day: the day we first heard about the murders. I left Alice still seething with fury and sorrow, I knew how she felt – they were my feelings exactly!

When I entered my home I had the usual nudge of anxiety, but it was unnecessary. I found my grandmother safely dozing on the sofa. For the first time since this nightmare began I was glad. Glad she did not have to face 'the world fit for heroes' which so many of her generation had given their lives to build.

Freedom is a wonderful gift, but like every thing created for good, in the wrong hands it is manipulated and twisted into evil.

As I looked at Gran she looked so peaceful, so innocent – like a sleeping child, and for once the comparison was not painful. There was a faint smile on her face that told me she was dreaming, and it was good.

She was obviously in a much better place: one safely beyond the ills of this world. Then I had the fantastic thought that perhaps Alzheimer's wasn't all bad, at least for its "victim." As a carer I had a different perspective, but maybe I could change my viewpoint.

I took one brief glance, one last thought, turned away and left her to her own brave new world.

BETSY

Gladys hung on long enough to receive her telegram – proving when the body is weak, the spirit is stronger.

We had planned a celebration and a recital of the next chapter in her unwritten book. Neither happened.

She passed on the same day, soon after a nurse had read aloud the words she had so much wanted to receive. I have learnt dying people will cling to life, often without knowing the reason themselves.

I think in Gladys' case she knew exactly what she was waiting for. She had been born in the reign of one queen, and died in the reign of another. She would have approved: she always claimed that queens make better monarchs than kings. After all, she argued, women are the homemakers, and what is a country if it is not a home. OK it may be a vast "palace" of an household, but what is more appropriate for a queen.

As you might expect, when she left no help was needed, she knew where she was going, but she stopped off to give me a parting piece of good advice.

I wonder now if she had some psychic inkling of the future – the very near future. Unfortunately I either chose to forget her words or, stupidly, made the mistake, I have so often criticised in others, of having a closed mind.

Either way it wasn't long before I was dealing with the fall out from my own bad choice.

Her advice had been short and sharp, and typical Gladys – nothing but the truth. She said to remember that just as there is always incredible goodness around us, but there is also pure evil. She added the warning: never forget both of these are hidden in the most unlikely people.

This isn't a very popular belief nowadays when we are encouraged to look for more acceptable explanations of unacceptable behaviour. Maybe that's why I ignored her caution.

About a month later I found this out for myself and along with it the answer to a much earlier question.

One evening I was surprised – yes I was still capable of that emotion – to see a young girl walking along the hospital corridor and at her heels skipped a small Jack Russell terrier. Without checking hospital regulations I knew these were spirits. Not ghosts, ghosts imply separate creatures who inhabit their own world and usually don't interact with ours.

This was definitely not the case – the young girl (I would put her at about fifteen) was looking at me and heading directly towards me. The dog acknowledged my presence with a soft growl, but it was half hearted with no real hostility in it.

For the first time since my new life began I felt anxious, a feeling usually reserved for mere mortals. I had grown used to death in all its forms, at least I thought I had. What I would encounter with this girl and her dog was the worst sort of human perversion – cold blooded murder.

The girl, obviously well brought up, introduced herself as Emma, and her lively little companion as Bob.

In these circumstances such formality would normally have seemed comical but Emma, for a young soul, was unusually serious and mature. As if she had seen too much misery in her short life. I was wrong. She had had a loving home and happy life – until the last few hours.

She wanted my help, but not the usual kind. She knew exactly where to go, and she knew she could take Bob with her. It seems the afterlife is not so finicky about fur, feathers and fins as we superior beings. All Heaven requires is good soul – the size and intellect of its temporary home has nothing to do with it. We have no decision in our birth, but it is important that we make the most of what we are given.

Emma had done a good job so far, but this night someone else's uncontrolled desires took away all her future hopes and plans. The fact it was done with such chilling, and practised, calculation gives no room for mercy. Emma had been his tenth victim. In destroying her body he had unintentionally set her free. She was making her own choice, and like Susan, it was an unselfish one. She could go on – that would be the easy decision, but it was not the right one. Not if you had a good conscience – Emma did.

Following in Joan and Gladys' footsteps I began walking along the corridor – in no particular direction. I had come to realise that walking is a great companion to talking. In our state you cannot actually claim it is good exercise, but It is an activity which avoids the awkwardness of face to face conversation.

So as we three walked, or bounced, along the corridor she told me their story and I understood why she couldn't leave. There was unfinished business.

She had been the victim of a sadistic serial killer. Emma was walking Bob when she was attacked and stunned by a blow as her stalker came up behind her. Bob, showing all faithfulness of his species put up a valiant defence. But he was no match for the carving knife their assailant carried. With her small guardian whimpering out his last breaths on the grass Emma tried to scream. But the gutless bastard had the advantage of surprise and strength: within minutes she was gagged and thrown into a nearby car. She was the tenth young occupant of its foul smelling boot. It was always a one way journey.

His method was always the same, and it was always planned to the smallest detail.

He would select and stalk his intended victim for several days, until he knew her routine. It was always a young slight girl – such predators are also cowards – preying on the vulnerable. Then one dark evening he would overpower her and cram her into his waiting vehicle. There would be a short drive to an isolated spot, where the terrified and confused girl would be raped and murdered. If she was lucky a few well placed knife thrusts ended the ordeal, if not – I will leave the sordid details to the more enthusiastic pens of our local and national press.

Thankfully Emma was too stunned to remember much and lost consciousness as the first blow cut into her lung. The last thoughts of her dying brain were for others: her parents and her faithful little dog.

She closed her eyes and when, seconds later, she reopened them Bob was there, gently licking her hand. But it wasn't the pulseless hand lying on the dark stained grass: the hand which just a few hours ago had stroked and cuddled Bob.

Emma knew that she was dead – even before she saw her killer effortlessly pick up her body and dump it back in the car boot.

Either through some lingering attachment to her body, or curiosity, she and Bob sat in the back seat while their murderer drove off. She wondered if he could sense them – it appeared not until Bob gave a deep growl and everything happened at once.

The killer looked quickly into the rear view mirror, and for a second his reflected eyes locked with Emma's. That he saw her was obvious from the terror in that look. Just a brief distraction but enough at a critical twist in the country lane. He swerved, then tried to straightened up, but over compensated and the car began a slow motion roll – well that's how it appeared to Emma, who was now watching from the verge with Bob sitting mesmerised at her side.

The car performed a complete 180 degree turn before being stopped by a sturdy oak, which was fortunately too old to be much bothered by the impact. It had seen many generations of foot, horse drawn and motortransport and would live to witness whatever else came along. Not so its attacker, which was an obvious write off.

Emma explained that all these thoughts passed

through her mind while she waited to see what happened next.

In fact it was a police car coming back from a burglary call out who were first at scene. From their initial assessment they were unperturbed about a spectacular, but not unusual, road traffic accident at a notorious bend. But as their next observation was a body hanging half out of the open boot this attitude changed rather rapidly.

All due process was followed: the scene was taped off and the lane soon filled with blue flashing lights and uniforms. Two of these were ambulances and their crews, who were equally perplexed, but professional enough to deal quickly with the two casualties. Here killer and victim went their separate ways: he now lay under the bright lights of an operating theatre, whilst her body rested in the darkness of our old friend, the morgue.

Hardly seemed right that he was surrounded by "carers" whilst she was alone: waiting to break her parents' hearts.

As we kept aimlessly walking it became clear that Emma was not seeking revenge or even justice: she wanted protection. Not for herself, she was beyond harm. No her only thought was to safeguard any more future victims.

I know they say that judgement, and punishment, is for a higher authority, but his choices had put Emma and her nine predecessors in an early grave.

Therefore was it only fair that our free will would return the favour. I agreed, and there was only one way: the serial killer would never leave the hospital.

Between us, on our third circuit of the hospital

corridors, we came up with a plan. There is always a plan.

It was a good one because it played to his weaknesses – there was a certain satisfaction in using this against him, just as he had done against others…

The first move was to find him: Emma and Bob could not be part of this.

Most killers are, by their perverted nature, selfish, they like to think of their victims as they left them – dead. If he saw her now, more alive than when living, he would be angry and suspicious. That was the last thing I needed.

I wanted him to be as unprepared as Emma when. a few hours earlier, she put the lead on Bob and set off for their earthly last walk.

We finalised our arrangements as we reached a junction in the corridor.

A few seconds later we wished each other luck and parted company. I watched the pair as they walked off – they had their own affairs to attend to.

I began to put our scheme into action, which must start by tracking down the murderer. I guessed he would be somewhere nearby – this experience would be strange for him. He would, hopefully, still be confused and remain close to the security of his body. In any case I doubted he would stray far from the source of his physical pleasures, because that's all he had.

So I began with a visit to the operating theatre and there found his body surrounded by a horde of medical staff and all the technology available to save his life . There was a 50/50 chance of his survival – according to the surgeon: odds which I am planning to change.

But of his spirit there was no sign – perhaps he had none! Maybe he would go straight to Hell! It may not seem a very Christian attitude, but I really hoped so.

Ah, if wishes were horses beggars would ride, and unfortunately I soon found myself on foot and stalking him around the hospital. Even in these circumstances I could see the funny side of that!

One thing I did find in the operating theatre was plenty of information. Like the morgue the place held an attraction for those perched between life and death.

Probably for the same morbid reason, but in this instance the patient was already notorious.

People are the same everywhere, and interest in our neighbours doesn't immediately cease in our 'halfway house'. Perhaps once we have passed on it may be different, but I hope not. One of the greatest joys of human nature is our fascination with each other.

The events of the accident and the arrival of the two casualties was the talk of our 'waiting room ' grapevine. Many claimed to have already come across the new patient.

All witnesses agreed with the warning Emma had given me. He was on the surface a most charming young man: late twenties, well dressed and groomed: almost too perfect. That was the only genuine thing about him: he was too good to be true. It was easy to see why he had escaped suspicion.

After all why would such a good looking, presentable young man need to resort to rape and murder. But rape is not about sex, it is about brutality and control. Murder is just the next step.

As I said before, in our world, the physical body cannot hide what lies beneath, and no one liked what they sensed within him. From what I could gather it was impossible to stay around him for long. As I followed his trail, I learnt more about him and one fact became clear. I was dealing with something I had never come across before…

No one could put it into words, except to say there was a "foulness" about him. Darren, a writer, and one of my new coma patients, came the closest. when he described his encounter as "like being suffocated by evil." He felt he would prefer to die rather than breathe the same poisonous air.

Which was an odd way of putting it because in this state breathing, as we knew it, is redundant – along with our lungs. None of this made me feel very enthusiastic about my forthcoming encounter, but I knew I was going to have to experience it for myself. I owed it to Emma and all the other girls, but more especially to prevent any further deaths. I also owed it to one small dog named Bob.

As I followed in his footsteps I began to realise I had underestimated him. Murderers are arrogant, they believe they are cleverer than the rest of us: they think they are untouchable. So he wasn't concerned about his own body, he was more interested in another corpse – one he had created. I knew, with disgust, where he was heading. He was going to the morgue.

As I drew closer I began to sense what the others had talked about. I have lived long enough to know the smell of rotting human flesh, it is a scent which lingers in your nostrils and is never completely forgotten. I recognised that odd sickly sweet stench now, and I knew it had nothing to do with the nearby mortuary.

Automatically I tried to hold the breath I no longer needed. Almost ninety years of habit is hard to break! I reached the morgue door, and paused: aware only it shielded me from the thing on the other side. I never thought of it as a human being: it was a nameless abomination. I took a mental deep gulp of air, and stepped through.

All my information had been right: not even the greatest writer could have put such emotions into words. I certainly couldn't, but I understood what Darren meant about choosing death above a much worse fate…

I was born with a gift, or curse, depending how you look at it. It is simply that I always get a very strong premonition from first meetings. I have tried to be practical and tried not to make quick judgments based on these 'first impressions'. But over the years these feelings have never been wrong, and in the end I have come to trust my gut instincts.

What I saw was exactly as everyone had described: what I felt was another matter.

I don't know what dreadful sickness it carried under its perfect skin, but Gladys words suddenly came back to me. What I was seeing and sensing was pure evil and it was more than life threatening, it was soul destroying.

But I had to deal with it, so I did – from as far away as I reasonably could.

I tried not to think of what I felt: push it to the back of my mind. In the hope if I did he would not notice how stomach churning I found his presence.

I need not have worried he was too involved in his own pleasure, which at the moment was trying to find a body – Emma's.Forgive me I actually helped him.

As I searched through the identification tags I felt my hands shaking: I couldn't tell if it was with nerves or barely controlled anger.

I should explain, just as we walk through doors in this state, we can also 'see' through them, and even locked steel freezers present no obstruction to this second sight.

I found her. As I stared down at the young innocent face, from which everything in this life had been taken, an overwhelming sense of waste suddenly hit me. Not just for this one girl, not just in this one place, but for all past lives he had stolen, and their loved ones. This gloating brute standing next to me – not too close – had changed everything. He had taken Emma's future, but he had also ruined the lives of everyone who loved her – they would never be the same.

I know we are told it is not our place to condemn, and that everything is said to be part of God's greater plan. But possibly I was part of that plan. Right or wrong I knew I was not going to stand over any more of his victims when I could have done something about it. I might have many sins on my conscience, but that would not be one of them.

There would be no regrets. I would answer for my own actions later, now I had work to do.

Suddenly I realised he was talking to me and, for

a moment, I wondered if he was using me as some sort of priest confessor. That would have been bad enough, but, no, he wasn't seeking forgiveness – he was expecting praise.

Excuse my French, but the arrogant bugger was actually bragging about killing Emma, and taking great pride in his handiwork.I almost took an automatic step back, then stopped myself. He must not get any inkling of how much I hated him. I need not have worried.

If he thought about me at all it was as an old codger, waiting to die and taking up valuable space while I did so. As a female, as he had proved tonight, I was even more disposable, but I still had one use which would keep me safe. He couldn't harm me in the usual way, but, without being over dramatic, there was something much more precious than my life at stake.

What protected me was his weakness: his obsession with self. All sadistic bullies need an audience and, like it or not, I was it.

It served my purpose. All I had to do was watch his performance and applaud at the appropriate moments.

Just keep him distracted for a short while. It should be easy.

It was the hardest and most unpleasant time of my long life.

Finally, after what seemed like hours, I heard a noise and the door opened behind me.

A hospital trolley entered being pushed by a couple of porters. These two were talking in hushed tones – but I felt not out of respect to their passenger.

Perhaps, even they, could sense the putrid atmosphere they had walked into. They deposited their burden in its refrigerated cabinet and left quickly, locking us both in. It no longer matters to me: by this stage locks cannot keep me out, and they certainly will not keep me locked in with this thing. That's at least one advantage I have: I doubt my companion has had time to learn that particular out of body skill yet. In fact I am sure he hasn't judging by his long walk here.

We are both silent, although, in human terms, so far I have barely breathed, let alone spoken. My companion has, thankfully, at last shut up. We are both staring down at the new arrival: he is shocked, I am fascinated. I have many more conflicting emotions: mainly the basic ancient urge to fight or flee.

Before I make up my mind I realise that I have company. Then I hear a low growl and know who it is. Emma and Bob have returned, and decision made: I am not leaving them alone with their murderer.

I did claim earlier no one has ever found out about their death by finding their corpse in the morgue. Actually, I'll admit that was not quite true.

Our fragrant friend is still absorbed with himself, or rather with what he once was. Meanwhile I am still wondering what his response will be.

Another, more serious, growl from Bob breaks the spell and the killer spins round to confront the three of us.

I am prepared for anything, except for what actually happens.

I hear a scream and wonder who it is – I even wonder if it's me!

Then I understand, and his screaming is far worse than anything else I could have imagined.

He was cold blooded about the idea of murder, but when confronted with his own mortal remains all pretence of sanity vanished.

His odour was horrendous, but his voice was so agonizing that I swear I felt my ear lobes curling up to act as plugs. A scream is bad enough, but his had such an appalling animal quality even Bob forgot his aggression and began to howl in harmony. For a few seconds all was chaos. Emma and I were both shocked into silence by this primitive display of emotion.

Then it all stopped as quickly as it had begun.

The four of us just stood still as the last sounds echoed around the metal filled room. As they died away I just continued staring ahead.

It reminded me of the past, when I had visited my grandmother in the asylum.

There were certain violent patients whose eye contact you always avoided.

You were warned not to look at them because in their mental condition the slightest movement could trigger a rage.

This felt exactly the same. We were shut in a room with a maniac who had completely lost any ability to control his emotions. I had one consolation.

I knew that three of us could escape: when Emma and Bob entered the room they had not used the door. Either Emma was a quick learner, or Bob's natural instincts had guided her.

While I was still planning our escape route I noticed something out of the corner of my eye. Just a slight movement, something I would probably have missed, except it came from the direction of our "friend." I turned my head slightly to confirm with both eyes what I thought I saw – or rather didn't see.

I didn't see him any more – put simply, he had vanished!

The remaining three of us broke the silence together:

Emma and I asked the same question in our different ways. She, a little uneasily, with the remark "Where has he gone?" While I, more to the point, came out with "What the Hell happened to him?" Bob was the only one who showed his immediate approval by jumping around us yapping excitedly.

There was no answer except he had gone – or been taken.

Perhaps my question had more truth in it than I imagined!

What if there is a parallel version of our corridor, but at the end of it there is no bright light, just a black pit. Then again what if there is no Hell, but an actual limbo where the evil go: unable to join the dead, or harm the living. I have also heard it said Hell is being excluded from the love of God's presence. Although I don't think that would be much punishment for those who had always chosen to hate. No I preferred the hellfire and brimstone idea, with the occasional pitchfork up the bum for good measure!

With this satisfying picture in my mind I suddenly remembered Emma and Bob. They were fine and busy: searching and sniffing around the room for any sign of after life.

So I sensibly decided, did it really matter where

he had gone, as long as he was no longer here! And he wasn't, that much was obvious from one thing.

The air, even for a morgue, smelled almost pleasant in an antiseptic way.

He had at least had the decency to take his reek with him. I hoped it would mix nicely with the sulphur!

It had all ended well, except for some lingering debate between the operating room staff.

It was some time later, while we were in the relatives' room, waiting for the arrival of her parents, when Emma told her story, or rather Bob's.

They had left me and gone straight to the operating theatre – an appropriate name since what was to happen there was a well rehearsed drama. They watched from a safe distance as he left his body and later saw me follow him.

Apparently the operation had been going well – too well for our liking – when there had been some sort of incident.

One of the surgical team had slipped, which would not have been a problem, had she not been standing next to the surgeon at the time. Neither would it have mattered had he not been undertaking the most sensitive part of the procedure – involving a scalpel.

As it was the outcome was fatal. The instrument which was intended to save a life in fact ended it.

All sorts of things were blamed: over zealous cleaning; under zealous cleaning; faulty footwear. An anaesthetist with an interest in psychology, even suggested a sub conscious desire not to save this particular life. There would no doubt be some sort of inquiry, where I am sure everyone would give their personal version of events. Except perhaps the shaken and slightly bruised nurse, what would she say: certainly not the truth.

After all who would believe it?

It was so bizarre even she would eventually be convinced by her own lie, but right now she knew what had happened.

She did not slip: she was tripped. In that split crucial second she had seen a small dark shadow cross in front of her feet – not only seen it, but felt it. A small, furry body.

And there was something more. After her 'accident' and before she was helped to her feet, for a few moments she was spread eagled on the floor.

While lying there, she would have sworn on a stack of bibles, she heard a gentle panting, followed by a warm damp touch on her face. Exactly like the lick of a gentle little dog.

Bob was, for a terrier, very well-behaved, and was always keen to please his young mistress. So it had been a good plan and easily carried out.

As we sat there silently congratulating ourselves, we agreed only one thing would have made this perfect. We both really missed the little physical comforts. One of those was a very English answer for every situation – a good old cup of tea.

As we parted in the early hours of another day it never even entered our heads this was not over.

Chapter Twelve

1992

ELIZABETH

1992 – Designated International Space Year. On the plus side : it sees the opening in France of the Euro Disney complex; the summer Olympic Games in Barcelona.

On the feminist side: Betty Boothroyd becomes first woman speaker in the House of Commons and the Church of England votes to allow women priests.

On the minus side: the bloody tangle of the Bosnian war begins; Los Angeles is devastated by riots following the Rodney King episode, and in the UK a fire in Windsor Castle causes £50 million damage; You will not find any of these events mentioned in my journal, except perhaps one.

In the Queen's Christmas message she referred to the year as Annus horribilus, somehow that must have rung a bell with me, because I have included this in my diary. Perhaps because I knew exactly how she felt.

OK, I did not own a castle, let alone one which had been devastated by fire, nor suffered the very public separation of my son and his wife. I didn't have to put up with newspaper headlines which vilified me, without being able to give a response.

I certainly wasn't one of the richest people in the land, but I didn't have the responsibilities which go with that. I also didn't have every spoken word or facial expression put under a critical microscope for display in the press.

But I did feel misunderstood, helpless and under threat. 1992 was a horrible year for me too.So what happened between 1st January, with all its positive new year pledges, and 31st December?

Well, for one thing, I don't believe in making promises you will never keep: it's just setting yourself up for failure. So I made no resolutions at the beginning of 1992. What was the point?

The main change was the grandmother I knew had virtually disappeared: by that last Christmas I remember taking a hard look at her and seeing none of the personality I loved.

She had lost all resemblance of an individual and taken on the vacant look you see in every psychiatric hospital around the country. The one they seem to use in zombie films to depict death after life. If I am honest now, and there's little point in lying, she frightened me.

I am not sure if the fear was for her, me, or both of us. Although she seemed to sleep more and more she still had moments of activity, which were increasingly irrational. What had formerly resembled childish pranks had now become something more dangerous and destructive.

The innocent pursuit of welly wanging had given way to more furtive practices.

One of these was hiding objects: usually valuable or perishable, with unpleasant results.

Another, less messy, but more distressing, development was the continual accusations of theft. This seems to be a very common characteristic of senile dementia and comes under the heading "you always hurt the ones you love." Thankfully no one took her accusations seriously, but by this point I didn't care. If my friends believed it, then they weren't my friends. I had other feelings to deal with. The pain of knowing my grandmother had changed so much she believed me capable of stealing from her. The extra irony being: another family member was guilty of that offence.

Poor Alice became her main confidant since she could be ensnared over the garden fence. Fortunately Alice knew me better than it appeared my gran now did and took all the grievances with some sympathy and "a pinch of salt."

Another development was the curtailing of visits to my long-suffering neighbour. Owing to the unpredictability of my grandmother's behaviour the tea breaks became shorter and less frequent. But Alice, bless her soul, was not deterred and began calling in to see me, bearing gifts of cakes and pastries. If Gran was awake and rational, she had to run a gauntlet of personal comment, bordering on abuse. Alice had the patience of a saint and bore it all with an experience born of 'been there, done that.'

With her help I even managed a few hours' escape to just wander around the shops, or a local park – depending on the weather.

A friend in need is a friend indeed!

But there were good moments too: often submerged by the daily drudgery.

For one thing my mother cancelled her yearly visit and instead planned an Easter trip the following year.

Ever since that infamous holiday my mother had continued her annual pilgrimage back to her birthplace. As you might imagine the next year proved a less than happy reunion. I had plenty of time to worry and brood. My temper was near the edge, and as is usually the case, it took just one more thing to bring it all boiling over.

The last straw was an old and well practised art on my mother's part.

As I grew up, every time my grandmother became distressed, I would feel the finger pointing at me, but always safely out of Gran's vision.

"There you have upset her again – you will be the death of her" would be the cry. The origin of my grandmother's unhappiness was always the same: friction between the two people she loved most on this earth. A mother and daughter who were acting more and more like rival siblings – which I suppose is what we were in the eyes of the law.

But I was not that gullible young child any more, and I no longer believed the accusations. I was an adult and in no temper to continue taking the blame, so instead took the best line of defence. I counter attacked with the observation that Gran was seldom upset in my mother's absence – so who was the cause of all this grief?

The resulting confrontation was so bad we literally took it outside, into the garden, and away from Gran's hearing. There a lifetime of grievance spilled over: with my mother washing her hands of any responsibility. She never thought she had done anything wrong. Memory is a highly selective process, and the way she dealt with uncomfortable facts was to develop a case of severe amnesia. Where there is no recollection there is no remorse.

But I did come to some sort of acceptance – thanks to a very wise and practical woman: our church minister.

Reformed churches have always accepted women ministers as equals and Laura had been the minister of our local Congregational church for several years.

As a child my attendance had been regular, but barely noticeable in the last years. It didn't matter, Laura was one of those Christians who practice their faith more outside the building than in it. She had been a great, mainly untapped, resource over the past years. My own fault: I had been so wrapped up in my problems I didn't look for a solution to them! Just like forgiveness, help is almost impossible to give to someone who doesn't recognise they need it.

But she did give me two invaluable pieces of advice regarding my mother.

You may think it odd I still referred to her by that title, and in fact growing up she was always just Margaret. It was only in adult years I called her "mum" – deluding myself there was such a simple solution to salvaging that relationship.

Of course it didn't happen, all it did was change the word's meaning. For me 'mother' does not have any special significance. Mothers are just people: some are good, some are bad, most are a combination of the two. The word contains no sentiment, it is simply a biological description.

Laura understood and gave me the following short, but priceless, guidance: "she may be your mother but you don't have to like her."

Where this came from I don't know: her own mother and father were the most loving of parents.

It didn't matter how she acquired this insight, but it did matter that it gave me a sort of absolution.

For the first time I was free to look dispassionately at my mother. I could see her without the pain of the past, or expectations for the future: as if she were a stranger, which in many ways she was.

It allowed me to examine her without guilt, or the hindrance of personal emotion, and it brought me to a conclusion. Although I hated her behaviour, and would never understand her thinking, I still felt something. It was sadness, but not for me, and not as a daughter. The only person my mother really hurt was herself.

When Laura shared her second piece of wisdom it made no sense at the time.

What she tried to tell me, but I refused to believe, was that my mother was weak, but not in any physical sense. There is an expression for this which now sounds a bit old fashioned "lacking in moral fibre," A curious phrase "moral fibre," it just means the courage to do the right thing in difficult situations.

This could not be. My mother was nothing if not strong minded and the most uncompromising person I knew.

I had yet to learn that being tough on other people is not the same as being tough on yourself. It's bravery by proxy, and has been practised by political, religious and military leaders for centuries.

It wasn't I thought my mother perfect: after all she had not displayed much morality in the dealings with her mother, or myself. But this was different. In plain language we are talking about cowardice, and that is a very serious charge.

It would be the last week of my grandmother's life before my eyes were fully opened.

But for now I turn a page and travel back to autumn 1992, where there are other worries to face.

Despite the brain deterioration my grandmother's general health was always fairly good.

That's the irony of old age: you hang on to your mental faculties, or physical abilities – seldom both. So you have an even chance of either ending up aware you are trapped within your own useless body, or being able to move without any understanding of where you are going, or why. I cannot wait!

Of course my grandmother suffered all the usual aches and pains in a woman approaching ninety. But one night in October that changed.

I don't recall the day or evening being remarkable in any way, and my diary only records the night.

In fact, I found later, Gran had a bowel infection, but she was now incapable of dealing with this situation.

She seemed to have forgotten all the normal procedures, or we even had a toilet.

It started at around midnight, when I heard her moving around her bedroom and got up to investigate. She was in bed, but as soon as I entered her room the smell gave it away. She denied any knowledge, but it was easy to find the soiled knickers hidden in a dressing table drawer. You just had to follow your nose.

So began a bizarre game of hide and seek. Every half an hour or so, I would hear movement and try to intercept the underwear before it found its wayinto another hiding place.

There were no dreams that night – I didn't have time to reach a sufficient level of unconsciousness.

By the morning we were both exhausted from several hours of coping with diarrhoea, or its aftermath. Even the washing machine was close to breakdown.

It must have been bad because it necessitated a rare doctor's appointment.

Now all this may not sound like a blessing, but good things can come in strange packaging. Finally we saw another GP, who explained these were the final stages of Alzheimer's. It was obvious to him that I did not know about the diagnosis made many years earlier. It was on record, but the original practitioner had neglected to mention it and no one else had picked it up.

Now they did, and the wheels spun into motion. Within a week a psychiatric nurse made that disastrous home visit, and plans were made for one day a week respite care. The wheels of justice, and the social services, grind slow so it never happened, but I did at last receive full time carers allowance.

This lasted until March, but to add insult to injury, Gran died twelve hours before pension day. So one of my tasks, along with death and funeral arrangements was to return that week's money. She had, apparently, not lived long enough to earn it!

Christmas 1992 it dawned on me this may be our last one together.

BETSY

Christmas again, and as usual not a white one. I think I could count on one hand how many of those there have been in my lifetime.

I don't need any fingers at all to work out the number of holidays: Christmas, Easter and birthdays I have spent without Beth since her birth – none!

We are together now, sitting on the sofa while a video of "White Christmas" is playing on the t.v… Beth knows how much I love this film, but I am not watching it.

Neither is my grand daughter, she is looking at 'me' and I see a tear run down her cheek. I always used to tell her it was unlucky to cry on Christmas Day, but I don't think you will find that in any book of superstitions.

This will be our last Christmas together – I am glad. I can see myself as Beth must see me, and it is breaking the part of me which I used to call my heart.

I want this to end so badly.

Many years ago I read A Christmas Carol and suddenly one phrase comes to mind which sums up my feelings "Spirit, take me away from here".

I seem to get my wish: I feel a psychic tug and though I would dearly love to stay with Beth I cannot help her. Later, once she falls asleep, we will spend the last moments of this last Christmas together, but for now someone else needs me.

So I follow the spiritual pull and drift off feeling like one of Scrooge's restless phantoms.

So here I am – in the morgue. I have never understood why, when there is a perfectly good hospital chapel. The closest I can come to an answer is the chapel is for the comfort of the living. The dead need no reassurance – they know the truth.

Funerals serve the same purpose and seem important in all cultures, regardless of religion, or even lack of it. I'll agree they are valuable rituals for the release of grief, but they are for the benefit of the mourners. Because of this I sometimes feel the coffin. rather than the deceased. becomes the centre of attention. All too often it is about death when it should be about the celebration of life.

Call me selfish, but I hope that my funeral will be about me, and not what will be left inside an expensive, and soon to be rotting, wooden box. Waste of a good tree. I will not be there.

Anyway back to the morgue – again! For once its almost empty, except for a solitary figure. One I recognise but haven't seen for a while: Jenny.

After a brief greeting, she tells me that she has a problem. One, which in all her years as a "guide," she has never come across before.

They have a patient in the nursing home who cannot, or will not, cross over into her waiting room. Arthur, a man in his eighties, was admitted before Christmas and spends all his days awake, and all his nights fighting sleep.

When he does fall asleep it is like he is fighting something else: he tosses, turns and mumbles incoherently. It is like he is trapped in some recurrent nightmare.

I remember Susan and ask if this could be a similar situation.

Jenny says not. Of course she has consulted her friend about it and found there is a critical difference. It was Susan's choice not to use this escape into her dreams. In Arthur's case he wants to leave but it seems the pathway is blocked.

I don't know what help I can be, but agree to return to the nursing home with Jenny.

We arrive to absolute chaos. There appears to be some sort of revolt under way, completely at odds with the season of goodwill. I soon discover there are in fact two distinct groups involved: the living and the near dead.

Only the latter are able to see me and I am met at the door by a deputation of 'waiters' some of whom I remember from my earlier visit. Unfortunately because of my obvious age seniority I immediately find myself as the centre of attention and their complaints.

Leaving Susan to try and pacify this group I follow Jenny along the hallway and into the communal living room. Here I find the second gathering comprising visiting relatives, patients and staff. You would be hard pressed to imagine these people peacefully sharing a festive good will lunch a couple of hours earlier.

Fortunately, none of them can see me, and have their attention fully on either accusing or apologising to each other. Most of the residents are oblivious and sleeping happily in their chairs: well at least their bodies are!

In the middle of the room I see the cause of this kerfuffle. Arthur sits alone in an armchair, and despite the commotion around him, he is asleep!

But he is not at peace: he is trembling and I see tears falling through his closed eye lids. I take an empty chair next to him. As I sit by him I touch his hand, which he seems to sense because he stops his restless movement and begins to mumble. One word, but he repeats it over and over. It's a word I remember, I first heard it many years ago. A word with dark meaning, but it brings a sudden flash of light.

I know what is wrong. I also know I can't help Arthur, but there is someone who could, or there used to be. My brother Norman, but how do I contact him? I can think of only one way – find a messenger – I need someone who is dying…

Death never takes a holiday and Christmas is no different, so I ask Jenny, and sure enough upstairs, away from all this 'excitement' is just such a patient.

Will it work – I don't have a clue – but it's Arthur's best chance.

So I visit the bedside of ancient woman who has outlived all her nearest and dearest. With the fracas downstairs she is passing alone: having been temporarily abandoned by the duty nurse. Not quite alone, a figure stands at the foot of the bed watching her own death with complete disinterest

Gertrude has been 'waiting' for some time and is not at all surprised to see me at her death bed. We have met before, and she is more than happy to help – if she can.

Neither of us know what the future holds,

beyond the light, but she will do her best. I have the more difficult job: all I can do is wait.

In the meantime I have to go back to the hospital. There has been a fight in a local pub and one of the participants suffered a fractured skull from a beer bottle. Unfortunately he had a thin skull and the injury will prove fatal. More tidings of comfort and joy!

When I arrive I find my patient standing, holding his head and looking confused. Probably the lingering effects from the brain injury and excess of alcohol. His body has already been pronounced dead and is being prepared for identification by his loved ones. What a wonderful memory for every future Christmas Day!

It takes most of the evening to convince the young man of his own mortality, so it is almost 10 pm before I hand him over to a caring grandfather and watch them go on their way.

I am afraid I was less than my normal sympathetic self. I had made a silent promise to myself, and Beth, I would return home before midnight. It briefly crossed my mind that I was a little like Cinderella in the pantomime earlier playing on the hospital television.

It was all quiet and if I left now I would be able to stop off and apologise to Jenny for my failure and promise to return tomorrow. Perhaps, between the three of us, we could come up with another plan.

My return to the nursing home was a very different experience. All was quiet and the only illuminations were those from the television and the Christmas tree lights . The relatives have gone, the patients are safely in their beds, and the staff, I suspect, are having a post mortem over a cold mince pie and hot toddy.

The spirit of peace and good will has been restored.

So I am surprised when Jenny meets me in the dark and deserted front hallway with the information that Arthur has a visitor. My first reaction is 'what idiot would visit at such a time on Christmas night?' The next thought is more worrying. Could some irate relative have stayed behind, and at this very moment, be bullying the poor old man.

No time for good manners, we shoot straight up into Arthur's bedroom.

It's all very peaceful and quiet, not at all what we were trying to prepare ourselves to deal with. I was extremely relieved: I am not sure what we could have done. For a few seconds I was envisaging turning into a poltergeist and frightening the attacker away.

Arthur is sitting in one chair with his guest in the other, who has his back to us. They are deeply involved in conversation, and I am glad we 'spirits' cannot disturb them. Except suddenly Arthur looks up and he's not looking through Jenny or I, but straight at us.

With almost one movement we both look towards the bed and there, sleeping like a baby, is the other Arthur.

"Why are you so surprised" comes a question close to me, "you asked me to come didn't you Bess?"

It's a voice I haven't heard in many years, but I recognise its owner before I turn back to see him. My little brother, Norman, the only person to give me that pet name, and he hasn't changed a bit.

Yes he is our mystery visitor, and I realise although I hoped to see him, I never really expected it.

We have much to say to each other, but the only thing I manage to get out is "thank you." We hug each other and he feels so sturdy and warm.

Touch is often more expressive than words.

Although when Arthur whispered that one word to me I knew if I could reach Nin (my pet name for him) he would help. There is a bond between certain people which is almost sacred: old soldiers is one of them.

You see my brother was a soldier. He, like Arthur, was also a Japanese prisoner of war and spent four years in an hell hole known by the infamous word 'Changi'

I don't know what was said between the two old comrades, but there would be no more nightmares for Arthur. Sometimes its a case of facing your fears, and one way is by sharing them with someone who understands – like Norman.

He left soon afterwards. We had not exchanged many words, but we will very shortly have all the time in the next world to talk.

And, I, well I was left with the answer to another question.

Just before my brother disappeared he gave me that look of remembering something important, which he had almost forgotten. A bit like that American detective I used to watch on tv. His final words to me were a short message which meant a lot.

"By the way Joan sends her love." and, leaving me speechless. he was gone.

They do come back

Chapter Thirteen

Easter 1993

ELIZABETH

New Year comes around, and I open my 1993 diary, which remains mainly blank pages, and turn back to the beginning.

No resolutions, and this year I didn't even stay up to see it begin: let alone give it any welcome. Not even a first footing for my neighbour Alice. I went to bed early.

I didn't anticipate much to celebrate in the months ahead. I knew I would have to face some quite difficult and painful decisions. My grandmother's physical condition had finally caught up with her mental deterioration.

She seldom moved, which did give me more time for myself. But this was a double edged sword because it also provided more opportunity to think.

Alice came around to visit me since I am still concerned about leaving Gran alone, but for another reason.

She is so frail I fear a fall could be fatal. Its strange that even when we know death is inevitable and natural we still want to fight it.

When I am rational, and not emotional, I accept the situation, and even consider myself lucky. Since

Gran's bowel infection she has returned to her normal toilet routine. I have never had to deal with incontinence issues – that is one blessing not to be undervalued.

It is not always so easy to maintain some basic hygiene, and we have limited absolutions to strip down washes. This was following a traumatic bath time session, when having helped her in I could not get her out. It required an emergency 'phone call to Alice and our combined strengths to hoist her out.

Even then this was not a simple manoeuvre since it was like dealing with a large, uncooperative baby. Every time we began to lift she just went limp!

Gran was beyond the humour of the situation, but Alice and I could see the funny side. By the time we had extricated my grandmother – and ourselves – from the bath we were so exhausted we were almost hysterical. I remember we sat on the bathroom floor, once the mess was mopped up, and rocked with laughter.

The biggest worry for me was food, or lack of it. As a young girl in domestic service my grandmother loved cooking, and eating. It had been some time since she prepared any meals. The kitchen, with all its sharp implements, is not the safest place for anyone with a failing memory and shaky hands.

Nevertheless Gran's appetite remained healthy – for an octogenarian. Of course she didn't eat the same size portions, but she ate three meals a day and still enjoyed treats. Rich tea biscuits and boiled sweets were her favourites. Every bedtime, for as long as I could remember, she had a nightcap: a spoonful of sugar, mixed in hot water with a dash of brandy.

All that changed in the last few months.

Shortly after Christmas she began losing weight and I began to notice her meals were left unfinished. By Easter she didn't want to eat at all, and when she could be coaxed, didn't eat very much. She was becoming weak and really it should have been no surprise what happened next.

Again, given her condition, I don't know why this should bother me, except it felt she had given up and that made me frustrated and angry. Was it, selfish: not wanting her to leave me. If I am honest, yes, just a little.

I know, in my heart, it really isn't me she wants to leave, its her body. An increasingly fragile, but obstinate, article which has become a burden to everyone. It's been a long journey and I ought to be glad it is all coming to an end. Most of the time I am.

But the natural process is too long for my grandmother. Is she still in control, and taking matters into her own hands? Is there enough logic left in that confused brain to understand the consequence of starving herself? If so then she has chosen a fool proof method: short of forced feeding there is nothing I can do to stop her.

It's the first time I have to admit to myself she is dying. Oh you could come up with the old chestnut that we all began dying when we were born, but I have to face the reality and its harder than I thought. I thought it would be a blessing when it came: a relief. The fact is, I am still not ready.

Up until now I was too busy coping with the present to consider the end of the process.

In the first months of 1993 Gran was sinking

further back inside herself. She barely moved from the sofa. Time no longer bothered her, and she just slumped gazing ahead at the television, or down at her hands. There was no intelligence in her eyes: just the vacant stare which says no one is at home.

I, on the other hand, suddenly found I had more time.

There is never enough of that irreplaceable commodity. There are moments when time drags, but this is only an illusion created by our own impatience or misery. The clock may stop, but never time, it just keeps relentlessly moving on.

In the middle of March I understood this and time became the enemy. Not because it was dragging: just the opposite. There wasn't too much of it, there was too little and it was running out. Christmas was no sooner over than Easter eggs were in the shops and I was anticipating the arrival of my mother.

In some ways I was looking forward to the distraction and, yes I'll admit it, the company. A chance to take a break from reality. Maybe I could even pretend we are a close, loving family, just for a couple of weeks. My mother would be following her usual routine: spending a fortnight with us and then travelling to visit friends in Norfolk.

I made the classic mistake of thinking I could postpone my problems until the next day. I forgot, or chose to ignore, the fact that for all of us, eventually, tomorrow never comes. No one lives forever.

My mother arrived the Monday after Palm Sunday, and I could see from her shocked expression how much my grandmother had changed.

Normally such a visit would trigger some

reaction, some recognition, but not this time… Did it hurt my mother she had become a stranger – it must have. I felt a twinge of pity once more…

There was virtually no time to play happy families, because on Wednesday we all, including Gran, showed the first symptoms of a cold. Where the germ came from I have no clue: why should I. Even medics are still baffled by the mysteries of the common cold and are no nearer a cure.

Perhaps my mother incubated it in the nurturing, warm atmosphere of her transAtlantic flight, or maybe it came from a higher source. With hindsight I can see it was a blessing, wherever it began.

It was a memorable Easter – for all the wrong reasons! There was no celebration, we were too ill. The cold rapidly mutated into a persistent and exhausting cough. Easter Monday, the chocolate eggs remain untouched, and we are instead living on a diet of antibiotics.

A week later and the medication has at last taken effect. Even Gran seems to be on the road to recovery: so her daughter continues with the plan to visit her East Anglian friends. She does not intend to return: from there she will depart back to her home and family in the States.

We should have remembered, particularly with all the symbolism of Easter around us, never to count your chickens before they are hatched!

It doesn't take long: the next day Gran suffers a relapse.

There is nothing ominous at first: I get her out of bed and make some breakfast – as I do every morning. But I have lived with this illness a long time, and my grandmother a lifetime, so I know it is not just another day.

I am scared, helpless, and desperate.

While frantically trying to spoon feed her the scrambled egg, which I think will prolong her life, she gently pushes my hand away and whispers something so softly I can barely hear it. I wish I could pretend I had not, but the time for denial is over. I have to accept what my grandmother has just told me: I have to believe she knows what she is saying when she repeats those three little words "I am dying."

It's one of those moments which literally leave you cold. Your brain seems to freeze and you cease to function. So I do the only thing I can – I call Alice. Bless her, she is at the door within seconds, and taking control until I recover. It isn't long: my neighbour always has a steadying effect on me.

I follow her advice and the second telephone call of the day is to our GP's surgery. He arrives, even before Alice has boiled the kettle for the compulsory pot of tea, and I am relieved to see it is my old friend from the gastroenteritis episode.

He is a good doctor, but better than this, he is a good person, and one who has years of experience behind him. He does all the usual physical checks, which are probably unnecessary. He has dealt with countless cases of terminal illness before and, unlike many of his colleagues, knows when to accept the inevitable.

He gives his verdict as compassionately as he can: it could be a few hours, or a few days, but he confirms my grandmother's own diagnosis. She is dying.

Maybe it is his gentle manner, or simply hearing

the truth spoken aloud, but suddenly I am very calm and clear. I am aware Alice sits next to me, and it's good to feel her presence, but I no longer need her support. Where it comes from, I don't know or care, but all at once I feel a tremendous strength.

Perhaps its that elusive 'moral fibre' I mentioned earlier.

The doctor is also wise enough to understand there is only one priority left: to give us what dignity and help he can provide in these last hours or days. His advice is always worth listening to, and he suggests we should avoid transferring her to hospital, where treatment would extend her misery.

I don't need any time to think about it. She has spent the last, gruelling, ten years of her life at home. If Gran wants to die in her own home, so be it.

He is as good as his word. For her remaining time: during most of which she is heavily sedated, he and his staff never lapse in their respect and care for her as an individual. It may be the old under funded and over stretched N.H.S., but no money on this earth could have bought the love and dedication we all received in the remaining time.

The doctor left with the promise to despatch his practice nurse within the hour to work out a care routine for Gran. He also gave me a private line to the surgery in the event I needed emergency assistance.

With our immediate physical needs settled, I made a third 'phone call. This time the visitor was Laura, who, as I expected, gave no glib theological sermons about forbearance and acceptance. But she did pray for us all, while she cuddled Gran in her arms, like the baby she had become.

Afterwards Laura talked about what we felt, and confirmed what we hoped.

While she didn't exactly advocate euthanasia, she did have compassion for those who did. She certainly didn't have any empathy with those intent on keeping people alive for the sake of it. Despite her disillusionment with this life, she had absolutely no doubt at all about an afterlife. She said she had spent too much time with the dying to leave any room for disbelief. She left us with what every spiritual leader should, but seldom does, understanding and confidence. She also left behind another telephone lifeline.

Now I have one final call to make. I have saved it for no other reason than I needed to deal with my own grief before I could deal with another's. I take a deep breath, pick up the receiver and dial a number beginning with a Norfolk code.

The conversation is brief and my mother agrees to come home straight away.

Then, for the first time in her life, she confides in me, and I rather think this is a mistake. A private thought unconsciously spoken aloud. But in one way it is another blessing. For the first time in my life, I really see her as a human being with all the flaws of that condition. Just as I had exchanged the adult role with my grandmother, I now feel I am doing so with my mother.

She told me she doesn't want to face this ordeal, with the unspoken wish that she would rather go home. She really has no choice: this time she cannot run away.

Suddenly the truth hits me like the shock of a

sledgehammer: Laura was right all along. I refused to believe her at the time. In the words of my mother's adopted homeland: I always thought she was 'one tough cookie'. But now I understood: to put it cruelly, she is a coward. Oh not in the sense of adrenalin fuelled bravado, but she lacks the kind of courage which calmly turns and confronts painful situations.

As, Laura tried to tell me, my mother had always avoided making any difficult choices: she preferred to take the easy way out and leave. First her daughter and then her mother. It also explained the way she dealt with the matter of my grandmother's savings and will. But I didn't hate her. Some people seem to be born with a nature, which no amount of nurturing will change. My mother was lucky to be born to the best parents in the world. The tragedy is her failure to appreciate her good fortune.

I put the receiver back on its cradle and break a connection which was never really made.

I turn my attention to my grandmother, who now seems to be involved in a conversation with her own grandmother, who has been dead for half a century. She died at the age of eighty seven, the same age Gran has always predicted for her own death. My grandmother unknowingly celebrated that birthday last September.

The doorbell rings once more. Our house is beginning to have all the peace and quiet of Paddington Station on a bank holiday. This time it is the district nurse, Mo, who is one of those professional angels, who takes control without taking away independence.

She immediately sets about organising what we need, not to make her life easier, but ours. The plan is for my grandmother to spend as much time with her family and friends as her illness allows. To facilitate this a whole team of nurses has been mobilised to deal with the more unpleasant tasks of care.

But for the moment Mo's priority is her patient, and her only aim is to make her comfortable. She does not make her own decision on this, but leaves the choice to Gran.

She asks to go back to bed.

Mo suggests we leave my grandmother with the trusty Alice and I show her upstairs. There she opens the mysterious holdall she brought with her and pulls out its contents. I recognise a folded piece of waterproof sheeting, but

I am a little surprised to see this followed by a comfortable soft fleecy under blanket. She strips the bed and sets about remaking it.

Mo does all this with the loving care of a dear friend or relative, rather than someone who was a stranger up until a few minutes ago.

When the job is done, to a nurse's satisfaction, the three of us help guide my grandmother back upstairs to her bedroom.

She will never leave it again.

So begins what is to be the last week of our life together.

BETSY

It's been a busy time at the hospital since Christmas.

The cold damp weather of the new year always provide a breeding ground for germs, which takes its toll on the elderly and vulnerable. The plus side for me was the old usually require little, if any, assistance to find their way.

In quieter moments I walk the corridors alone and it seems a long time since I had company. True, I always have a group of 'waiters,' but they are a fleeting bunch. They provide entertainment, but not companionship. Besides most of my long term guests spend their 'out of body' time exploring their new world. I don't blame them: after my relationship with Joan I am not keen to form any more close bonds. Cutting them is too painful.

Then I remember my other brother Jack, who told me of his wartime life in the R.A.F. The losses were so great they avoided any familiarity with replacement crew, since any friendship would be short lived.

I envy the stream of souls passing by me, they will soon be with their nearest and dearest. This is especially true when I see someone I know, and at my age this is inevitable. There are so many people who have gone before me, and want to be with them. As if everyone else is going to a party, to which I am not invited. I feel I belong with them. I have no place in this, bodily preoccupied, world, when mine has outlived its usefulness.

The meeting with my brother has made me realise how much I miss all my family and friends. How much I miss my Grandmother, and George.

But time passes slowly when you have idle hands, so I try and keep occupied.

Sometimes I feel as if I am running some sort of afterlife citizens advice bureau: helping those who need it – even if they don't always appreciate it.

There are so many questions, and I have too few answers. For one thing I remain virtually ignorant about what lies beyond the light.

When I am bored, and feeling poetic, I imagine our corridor like a stream which joins with other streams to form a vast river of souls – all meeting together with the newly dead around the globe. They are moving towards a sea which has no prejudice against any religious, or spiritual belief. Its values are not set in stone, written on paper, or lectured from a pulpit. They are the virtues of honesty, generosity, kindness, patience, and above all, love.

But thankfully I have very little time for imagination. Business is brisk. Just like undertakers I am guaranteed an endless supply of customers. Nothing much changes except faces and stories. Death is relentless: whether accident, sickness or suicide. Fortunately, though, no more murders have come my way.

By a natural train of thought my mind goes back to our serial killer. I know his name, but will not give him the fame he committed multiple murder to obtain.

Lets just call him Jack. No offence to Jacks in general, or my brother in particular. It just seems appropriate our killer should share his nickname with an earlier monster. Another coward who stalked his victims over a century ago – in the streets of Whitechapel – so Jack it is.

Since that night I have neither seen nor heard any sign of our 'Jack.' Not that I am looking for any!

But I have seen Emma and Bob: in fact I see them almost every evening.

They are the exception to my rule about friendships. In any case it is too late for warning: we were close from the moment we met.

Most nights I see the pair walking around the hospital grounds, almost as though they are trying to finish the walk they began so many months ago.

Afterwards they join me inside, where we continue to ramble through the familiar hospital corridors for a while. I am glad of the company and the conversation. We talk of many things: some trivial, some serious: but never mention Jack.

One of our frequent topics is Emma's decision to stay around: not that I am complaining, but I am curious. She always replies that she is happy and content. She is too young to have any strong ties to anyone in the other world and not old enough to have become jaded by life in this.

Surprising, considering the brutal way she left it. As for her faithful little companion. Well Bob's tail tells me all I need to know. His whole world revolves around his mistress, and he will follow her – wherever fate may take them. Again I feel a gentle prod of envy: unlike me, they have each other: they will never know loneliness. There is always a plan.

Then one evening: following a bitterly cold day in the middle of February, this comfortable routine changed. Although we cannot feel the misery, or pleasure, of extreme temperatures: established practice tends to keep us indoors in bad weather. So I did not expect to see my two friends outside in such inclement conditions.

But in fact I didn't see Emma and Bob at all that night.

Nor did I see them the following day, or the next. It is the fourth evening and I have been dealing with the casualties from a road accident. Only one vehicle involved, but five bodies lie in the morgue: three generations of a family wiped out by the deadly combination of wet roads and freezing air. Black ice I think they call it.

It's been a long, hard night: helping them come to terms with their deaths.

More difficult because I still have a problem understanding such tragedies myself. It isn't until midnight when I finally convince the grandparents to take their two year old grandson and his baby sister away to a 'better place.' Anywhere, I argue to myself, is better than lingering to witness a grief which they cannot comfort. I have kept them well clear of the morgue, and the bodies which are barely recognisable. But neither they, nor I, can persuade their son to join them. He is determined to await the arrival of his wife, even if just to see her one last time.

I do not attempt any more argument: I know

when I am beaten. So I do the only thing I can. I keep a young man company, who a few hours ago had everything to live for, and wonder how a compassionate god could rip it away from him.

Sometimes the explanation 'ours not to reason why' is not good enough.

Eventually, in the darkest hour, just before a feeble dawn, his wife arrives at the hospital, and I breath a sigh of relief, she is not alone. The couple who accompany her I would guess are her parents. What they are about to face is, thankfully, beyond my grasp.

How do you deal with such heartbreak? It puts your own problems in perspective. I feel grateful. and guilty at the same time, for thinking of myself in such terrible circumstances.

Mercifully, the young woman, who yesterday was a busy wife and mother, is too dazed to resist her parents' decision to deal with the ordeal of identification. Instead she is shepherded away by an older nurse, and we follow them.

We don't go very far before I realise where we are heading. It's a place I have been before.

The chapel appears deserted, as you might expect at this hour. Visitors are long gone, and all patients sleeping peacefully in the arms of Morpheus or morphine.

The four of us go and sit at the front of the small sanctuary. I realise there is a gentle irony in the fact the two women take up position on what would have been the bride's side of the chapel, while I sit with her husband on the right.

To add to the strangeness of the situation, there

is absolute silence: no weeping, no murmurs of sympathy. I would have said, before I knew better, as still as the grave.

This atmosphere is broken by a movement – but one only I can see. My companion has left me and sits on the other side of his wife, where he places his hand over hers. The nurse is oblivious to what is going on just a foot or so away, and I am from a generation where intimacy was just that – private.

So I look away.

I don't know whether it is an emotional reaction, or the still atmosphere of the chapel, but suddenly I find myself doing something I haven't done for ages: I pray. I am from a low church background, so there is no dramatic falling onto my knees. As taught by my grandmother, I quietly clasp my hands together, close my eyes, and send a silent message to God. Why is it that we usually only pray when we want something? I feel a bit awkward, I seem to be treating God like Father Christmas: sending a 'wish list' to heaven, with a promise of good behaviour.

What do I ask for? Sorry, this also comes under the heading 'personal and confidential.' But you could probably hazard a good guess for at least part of my requests.

I don't know how long I sit there, but when I open my eyes the seat next to me is once more occupied. My young friend has returned and answers one of my prayers in three little words: "I'm ready."

I begin to get up, but he gently puts his hand on my shoulder and says, "No, it's OK: I know the way." He doesn't say another word: just smiles and leaves without a backward look.

As he goes out the door he passes through a small group coming in. The formal identification is over and the parents are guided by the same young doctor who took them into the morgue. He looks uncomfortable. Poor soul, he has yet to find the balance between caring and coping: perhaps he never will. He may either end up leaving to save his own sanity, or developing a skin so thick nothing can pierce it, and he becomes a hardened professional worthless to his patients.

But for now he is struggling, and is only saved but the young widow hurrying up the short aisle to hug, and in turn, be hugged by her mother and father. They all leave together and I am alone.

I was about to turn back to the small altar, when something caught my eye. I realise I was wrong – I am not alone in the seemingly deserted chapel. There is a figure huddled in a corner almost hidden by the open door. .

My immediate thought is whether this person is one of us, or is he something else entirely. Somehow I know the creature is male, although I am not sure it is human. This thought brings an emotion I thought was long gone: fear.

All this passes through my mind in a few seconds: while the chapel door is swinging shut. As it does so its shadow slowly passes over the shape until my companion is completely revealed.

Someone I know, but had not thought, or hoped, to see again – Jack!

I am not a good liar, and even if I was, my facial expression would give me away. I am an open book which he can easily read.

But instead of gloating at my embarrassment he quietly says, "Please don't be scared, I am beyond hurting any one."

For the want of something more intelligent to say, I ask "What do you want from me?" Because as clearly as he can read my expression, I can read his.

He is here for a reason and its something, rightly or wrongly, he thinks I can give to him. I really hope I can. Not for any charitable reason, but so I can get rid of him. Although his distinctive aroma has virtually gone, there is something still disagreeable in the air around him.

Now it becomes clear why Emma and Bob have made themselves scarce in the last few days.

He goes on to answer a question I have not asked: although I have thought about it many times since his disappearance. He tells me where he has been since our last meeting in the morgue.

Apparently he was removed, the only way he can express it, to a small dark place. I suppose you could say it was a sort of limbo, but he describes it as like being in solitary confinement. I imagine with his background, he would know. But although he is alone in this 'cell' there are others in this awful place.

All around he hears the sound of other inmates. Some are unrepentant and shout, while others are terrified and scream. The resultant racket is unbearable, but it must be borne. Imagine a bare cube with no window, no door: no escape. Even worse there are no gaolers: no one to swear at, or plead with.

I once heard it said one of the cruellest forms of punishment was being thrown into a pit and left to die alone – forgotten. But what if you could not die?

Often, in my darkest moods, I have thought of Death as an eternity of nothingness. But what if Hell was an eternity of isolation. Tell me, honestly, which would be your preference. Do we really want to live forever without hope or love? Would the cost of 'life at any price' be too high?

I am still thinking about this when I realise Jack has asked the question I have been waiting for, "Please could you help me – I am so sorry for what I have done." I know very little about the theological belief in repentance – except I know it must be sincere. I seem to remember a Catholic priest saying so in a television drama – to receive absolution you must truly mean it.

Again he must see the doubt written on my face because he carries on "Let me tell you something about myself, and then maybe you can understand even if you cannot forgive."

Then we sit down, side by side, in a back pew and he tells me the story of his life. Its an old, and, sadly, not very original one – a childhood of constant abuse and cruelty. First at the hands of his drug and alcohol addicted parents and then a string of foster homes. Most of whom, he admits, were decent people, but the harm was done and he was already 'damaged goods.' Before his teens he had a peer group network which ensured no good influence would breach it. He never stayed long in any foster home.

Reading between the lines of his history, I guessed they either quickly saw he was a lost cause, or sensed something wrong about him. Perhaps they were wise. But I mentally shook off my suspicions: a sympathetic nature told me to give him the benefit of the doubt: my common sense warned me to beware.

In young adulthood, when he could legally make his own way, it was too late. He admitted he had made too many poor choices, most of them involving bad company.

I couldn't help interrupting him at this point. Yes, lack of care and love, combined with the 'wrong' friends, is usually a recipe for disaster – but not usually multiple murder. I didn't add the thought that serial killers are generally lone predators. Yes there are well-known cases of murdering twosomes, but I knew there was no accomplice in this case. He explained this easily enough: there was one crony in particular who had led him down this path. They might indeed have ended up partners in murder, except for the fatal combination of a bottle of vodka with a late night double decker bus.

Then he paused. No, he said, it was no one's fault but his own. He would not go down that route any more: blaming someone else to justify his own wickedness. Let God punish him however he wished – he deserved it. He did not deserve forgiveness. I have to admit, I agreed with him.

He stood up and went to the front of the chapel, shouting back at me, "Get out please – leave me alone."

I gladly did as I was told and went through the door. Immediately I heard a dreadful noise. It sounded like an animal, but was like nothing natural I had heard before. It was a primitive, ancient sound. Then I realised it was sobbing, which, incredibly, was more awful than the screaming I remembered from our last meeting.

Just like someone with a fear of heights being drawn to the edge of a cliff, I was pulled back into the chapel. I didn't want to go, but neither could I leave.

He was half kneeling, half lying, on the floor near the altar with its small effigy of a crucified Christ. This is not something I am comfortable with: coming from my Victorian upbringing and Congregational church background. Strong emotion and spiritual belief are both too private for public display. He is either genuine in his remorse, or giving an academy award worthy performance.

To be fair he doesn't know I have returned: but, to be cynical, he has proved himself an talented actor.

I have to ask a question – just one, but the answer will help me make probably the greatest decision of my life. So I ask it. "How did you get here?" He says that he doesn't really know. He remembers being curled up on the floor of his 'cell.' He doesn't know how long he had been there. It was too dark for vision to be much use, but all his other senses more than compensated. In fact he would happily have gone deaf too, if it meant he could no longer hear the tortured screams of his fellow damned.

He felt he was going mad: almost hoped so. But could someone lose their mind if they had no brain?

It the midst of these aimless ramblings another thought came to him, this one from a long stored memory.

Imagination can be blessing or curse. This time it was the former. It temporarily released him from the torment of his present to the happiness of his past.

One Christmas Eve when his grandmother had

taken him to Midnight Mass. The recollection was magical: shining bright decorations moving in the flickering lights. Everything seemed to have a life of its own. To his impressionable young mind, the solemn statues in the old church seemed to move. Even the figure of Christ seemed to be trying to break away from its enormous cross. This sounds like a scenario from a horror film, but Jack wasn't scared – he was fascinated.

The memory brought with it the seasonal scent of pine needles, hot candle wax and incense. It had been his one and only association with a church until now: his loving grandmother had died three months later. She departed with a final piece of advice: "You can always be forgiven, if you are truly sorry."

I have thought this is a bit of a cheat – like a "get out of jail free" card in the Monopoly games we played with the grandchildren. But I now realise it is not such a simple bargain for either party. Forgiveness and repentance are easy to preach, but hard to practice. For one thing, how do you know if you are truly sorry, let alone read someone else's conscience.

While these thoughts passed through my mind Jack finished his own reminiscences. As he dwelt in this forgotten moment from his past he said he was aware of a sudden change. He was no longer in total darkness: there was a small glimmer of light. Enough for him to think he had truly travelled back in time. He seemed to be in a miniature version of his childhood memory: he was in a church.

Actually he was in a corner of the hospital chapel, where I found him.

This explanation, although a bit dramatic for me, still touched a sensitive nerve, and for the first time I began to believe he was capable of telling the truth.

Suddenly, when I look at him I don't see evil disguised in human skin. I see the young innocent boy, I am now convinced, he once was.

Perhaps if his victims had still been around I might have had second thoughts, but Emma and Bob remained conspicuous by their absence. So, unbelievably, I found myself bending down and holding him, with no disgust or hesitation. I am amazed at myself – could this be real forgiveness, and do I have the right?

If I am wrong, if I am being foolishly gullible then so be it. I will have to leave justice to an all seeing, all knowing, God. And hope Emma will understand my weakness and excuse my betrayal. Bob I need not worry about: like all dogs his love is absolute and without reproach.

So here began a period of hard work – for me. My first charitable instinct didn't last beyond that evening: when I left Jack in the chapel. Over the next few days there were many times when my conviction of his sincerity faltered.

Moments when I thought I caught a glint of something not quite right in his eyes. Most of the incidents I could pass off as a trick of the light, or my natural suspicious nature, but I couldn't forget them.

Other times, and increasingly, I began to see another side to Jack. Part of my plan to help him, was an unofficial programme of helping others. So every evening I would meet him, in the chapel, and he would follow me on my rounds.

At these moments you could easily fool yourself he was a completely different person. Perhaps that's how my fellow waiters saw him: how they coped with his nightly intrusions into their world. They must have recognised him from news reports, but to give them their due, they never showed it. Maybe they were just displaying a well known national trait. Apart from an obsession with the weather, the British also have another quirk. Perhaps it comes from being an island race, but we have a tendency to keep our problems to ourselves and allow others to do the same. The famous stiff upper lip! This is not to say we are an unfeeling bunch, just a bit uncomfortable with strong emotion.

Anyway for just over a week Jack served his self imposed sentence with me. I sometimes wondered who was being punished!

During this time we helped many faced with the frightening and confusing reality of their own deaths. After a couple of days, when I began to trust Jack more, I left him alone with some of these souls. But never the young females: my faith wasn't that great, and I saw no point in putting temptation in his way, or danger in theirs. OK he could no longer harm their bodies, but I remembered how threatened I felt by our first encounter.

Besides I had another, less sympathetic reason, I wanted to learn what other people thought about my 'apprentice.'

Jack never accompanied me on the last stage of their journey. Perhaps it was one more indication of my continuing doubt: for some reason, I did not want to show him 'the corridor.' So this was a perfect opportunity for a little private chat.

Most of my companions never connected the friendly, good looking, young man with the scowling serial killer they had seen in their newspapers. Why would they? They had more immediate personal concerns: mainly their destination! Heaven or Hell. This indifference was valuable because it gave me their honest opinion about Jack. It was easy to drop him into the conversation during our final walk.

Indeed often they would bring him up themselves. One elderly man described him as a charming, caring character, who he would be proud to call 'son.'

But there was something about the description which bothered me, before I realised it was the word 'character.' It made me think of an actor playing a role.

This thought was pure instinct: irrational and illogical. I have been on this earth long enough to learn such feminine intuition is either treated with ridicule or suspicion. I seriously doubted matters would be any different in this halfway house. So I put the idea away: on the back shelf of my mind, and carried on with the job in hand.

Most of our regular waiters took their lead from me. At first they had justifiably been wary of our new member, but they tolerated him for my sake.

You see I had become a sort of cross between hospital matron and agony aunt: the font of good advice. Quite a responsibility, and one I hoped I was up to.

One thing I was wise enough to know: it would make life easier if I kept Jack busy and away from the others as much as possible. Of course this meant

I spent more time with him.- alone. I am neither a martyr, nor masochist: this was not as unpleasant as it sounds. It reminded me of Joan, and those last days she spent with James.

There was no comparison between the two young men, except on a physical level, but the memory of my old friend was always welcome. It brought with it a pleasure which was worth the cost. Happiness was in short supply at the moment and I would take it where I could.

The start of our third week and we had settled into a comfortable state of routine. I even considered the unthinkable. Jack's service as my replacement may also provide his salvation. He would not have been my choice, but perhaps he was God's. You see, by this stage I was under no doubt about the existence of some higher power.

The first of March, and it was mild enough for a lovely show of daffodils to celebrate St David's Day. Hope was in the air – all the scents we think of as Spring. It would have been perfect, except for my loss of Emma and Bob.

It didn't seem right such a day would be a time for tragedy, but fine weather and longer daylight provides more opportunity for adventure – and accidents! This was the case today.

A group of teenagers had taken advantage of the long awaited sunshine to take a cycle ride out to a local riverside beauty spot. You may guess what happened next. Youthful high spirits, combined with a sense of invulnerability, proved fatal, and by the end of the day there was a new resident in our morgue.

Vicky was a pretty young sixteen year old: at least

she had been before the muddy Thames distorted her features. She may have reached the age of consent, but was still innocent enough to see only the goodness around her.

She was everything I would have kept far away from Jack.

As it turned out there was no choice. We were together when she came: asking for our help.

I have no alternative but to lead the way to the one place I never wanted Jack to see… The corridor.

Of course I have never experienced the infamous final walk prisoners make on their way to execution, but I imagined it must look something like our small procession. I walked slightly ahead with Vicky and Jack following behind. No one spoke. At this point I was unsure whether I was the executioner or condemned.

We arrived at the well known spot, but Vicky seemed reluctant to continue.

Unbelievably she asked if one of us could go with her, and, before I could reply, Jack took her hand. They began their last journey down the corridor.

It's too late for me to do anything: Jack is dragging Vicky along behind him and they are almost to the light at the other end.

But there is something different about it, and I understand what it is: there is no one waiting.

Just before they reached the empty beam Jack turned, and for a moment I wonder if I have misjudged him, but then he shouted back to me. "You stupid old cow – did you really think you could convert me – just like my bitch of a mother, and all those other f'ing do gooders. You can't change me and you can't stop me." He pulled Vicky towards him, stepping backwards into the light, screaming words so violently I could barely understand them – "Well goodbye you silly old bag, you are just like all the other morons. You will never beat me because I am cleverer than any of you."

But Jack is wrong, he doesn't know everything, and he certainly doesn't know I met Vicky in the morgue earlier that evening, and we made a plan.

As I said, I have learnt to respect my instincts, they are never wrong. So it was a case of hoping for the best while preparing for the worst. This being the situation in front of me.

Several things happened at once, all triggered by my pre arranged signal to Vicky. A raised two finger gesture which has a variety of meanings. During the Second World War Churchill used it as a symbol for Victory: in recent years it became a sign for Peace. Reversed it has quite another meaning.

But in this case it could have suited any of the three.

As soon as Vicky saw it she reacted: she yanked her hand free from Jack's and threw herself back towards me and away from the light.

I have seen storms which instantly turn the sky from day to night and this is exactly what happened as Vicky dived to the floor. The halo of light vanished and was replaced by a black pit.

Neither Jack, nor Vicky, could see what was forming behind them. I was the only witness and I was incapable of speech or movement as I watched with dreadful fascination.

There was something in the darkness. It had eyes,

although I have seen no human, or animal, with orbs such an unhealthy shade of blood red! It was like some prehistoric thing saved from extinction: somehow still living. At least its black snakelike tentacles were very much alive as they fastened themselves around the nearest object – Jack. I watched as both creatures seemed to merge into one as the human body began writhing within its gyrating bonds. It was grotesque: like a puppet being twisted into anatomically impossible shapes.

All at once my paralysis of horror was broken as I saw a shape crawling towards me, from out of the darkness. A small human figure, and all else forgotten I dashed forward and pulled Vicky clear.

We staggered back to the protection of the other end of the corridor, although unconvinced anywhere was safe near that awful ancient force. Then we watched as the tortured soul, which had been Jack, began screaming as he was dragged slowly into the pit.

The screaming I remembered from the morgue was nothing compared to the inhuman death cry he now produced.

We both crouched down as though to avoid being sucked into the foul steaming sewer. We held each other, closed our eyes and waited until all was silent. When we looked up there was no darkness, no light: it was just a corridor. The supernatural storm had passed, and as in nature, the air felt fresh and clean.

I had been right. Jack had been playing a role: but something more important than a career depended upon its success – his very soul.

Unfortunately, for him, a higher and far better judge than I, found his performance wanting.

I remember once seeing a painting in a high church: probably during my Church of England school days. It showed St Michael weighing a soul for the Last Judgement. It was a good heavy soul so it tipped the scale and was sent to Heaven. Jack's soul was obviously too light and went in the opposite direction.

Proof of the famous statement by Abraham Lincoln: "You can fool all the people some of the time, and some of the people all the time, but you cannot fool all the people all the time."

I would add to this: God, you cannot fool at all.

I hate to appear wise after the event, but he didn't deceive me. Not because my intelligence was higher than anyone else's, but because Jack made the classic mistake of youth versus age. He saw only my useless ageing earthly body: he never saw the spirit beneath, with all its experience of one life, and increasing knowledge of the next.

This arrogance proved his downfall, because while he was concocting his plan, I was making my own.

I had planned for this eventuality from the beginning. I guessed, coward as he was, he would use another soul as a shield. So every one I took to the corridor had been briefed in case he attempted something like this. If Iwas wrong then no harm done, but if I was right? The thought that I would be the cause of such an unholy mistake was more than I wanted to consider.

So when I met Vicky I saw a chance to force the issue, and she was more than happy for one last adventure.

Perhaps it was unfair to put temptation in Jack's way, but I knew my time was growing short. Like most dying people I wanted to leave no unfinished business behind. Besides I rather hoped I was going to Heaven, and the last person I wanted to meet there was Jack.

The thought about my own mortality reminded me I needed to be somewhere else. So I gave Vicky a big hug and prepared to send her on her way, when I heard something. A small snuffling sound: as distinctive as an individual human voice, or a special little dog. I looked behind, and what I saw filled me with so much joy. Emma and Bob.

A general commotion followed, with Vicky joining in the celebration. The two girls had never met, but were bonded by age and a love of dogs. It was appropriate Emma should be the one to accompany her new friend to the light, so we said our goodbyes and I let them go.

As I watched the two figures, with little Bob skipping around their ankles, go down the corridor I felt happy for them, but sad for myself. I understood my time here was coming to an end, there would not be many more moments like this.

Chapter Fourteen

A week in April

ELIZABETH

It's been an extraordinary long week: time only distinguishable as night and day. The face of a clock barely matters any more, except for our visitors.

Doctors and nurses who arrive and depart like clockwork, to bring some sort of normalcy and life to our isolated little world preoccupied with death

Thankfully they are used to these situations, so the conversations they bring are never stifled with embarrassment. They understand the urgency for frankness, but need for compassion better than most. So they bring us what we need before we know it ourselves.

All my grandmother's medical, physical and human comforts are quickly attended to, with love and dignity. There is not enough time left to waste.

What remains for us to do?

Well they have made this clear too. Our 'job' is to spend whatever time remains together: not just for my grandmother's sake but for us all. There will always be regrets about the past, but perhaps these last moments, whether hours, days, minutes or seconds, will help our future.

In the first days of the final diagnosis our home

was a hive of activity. All Gran's remaining relatives and friends were notified and came to pay their respects. The bedroom buzzed with hushed chatter: not that Gran appeared to hear any of it, or perhaps she chose not to. She was heavily sedated. The doctors assured us she was in no physical pain, but mentally she appeared in torment. She would thrash around in a confused state: first wanting to get up and then sinking back in bed. The medication changed from sedatives to a stronger terminal drug: diamorphine.

We sometimes wondered why, for someone so resigned to dying, she fought so hard to live. Perhaps breathing was just a lifetime's addiction.

In the later stages we spent a lot of time wondering aloud if there was something keeping her here. Some unfinished business.

But in the first few days Mum and I were too busy making cups of tea, while our visitors provided the sympathy, to come up with an answer.

By mid week all calls ceased: I was not sorry. Although one nurse advised hearing was the last sense to go, I don't think Gran would have appreciated the depressing comments made by some of her guests. Mainly stating the sodding obvious. I know death nowadays is regarded somehow as an embarrassing failure, but really people could come up with something more original than "my word she does look ill." Not entirely fair since we did have a few callers who brought laughter from the past, rather than wallow in the present. These were mainly her own generation, who had a different, more practical, view to death. Probably because their own was not so far away.

By Thursday we were on our own, apart from our devoted nursing team.

It was an odd situation, two people so close they once shared a body, yet now finding it difficult to share a room. But we were always aware there was a third person nearby and kept conversation polite. To give us both credit, I think we would have done so anyway: a deathbed is not the place to try to settle selfish arguments.

However such intense shared intimacy could not fail to reach some sort of resolution. I would always be disappointed we would never live up to society's view of a devoted mother and daughter. But I could accept the fact, like many such relationships, this is a fallacy. Mother Nature has a more practical approach: it expects much less, and at the same time much more. While it demands the young should be protected, if necessary with the parents' lives, once the job is done both resume their independence. There are no long term expectations or guilt based on brief biological urges.

All we really require, once we have been pushed and pulled screaming into this world, is someone to love and nurture us. In this I was blessed. But everything has its price and now payment was due. Birth and death are opposite ends of every life. Both involve a love and pain which are inseparable: you cannot have one without the other and most of us are happy to accept the exchange. If I now had to face the grief of losing my grandmother so be it. There was nothing lacking in my life, so how could I feel resentment or anger against my mother.

The days and nights passed slowly: mum and I

ate to live, so meals were few and far between. On the other hand we acquired a strange addiction to tea and consumed gallons of it. I had not realised how long you could survive without food or drink, because neither passed my grandmother's lips the entire week. Her body was obviously growing weaker, but her spirit was still willing, because on Saturday evening a sort of miracle occurred.

Human beings adapt to seemingly impossible situations, and by the weekend we found ourselves settled into a routine.

During each day and night we would take turns, watching and sleeping, while Gran's favourite songs played on a small cassette player.

Luckily we had a good supply of Al Jolson and Bing Crosby tapes!

But every evening we would sit together on opposite sides of the bed, with Gran between us. There we would rejoin the outside world for a couple of hours: courtesy of a small portable television.

It was during this quiet shared moment on Saturday evening when Gran came back to us. I cannot know how much effort it cost her. It wasn't for very long, but enough time to say goodbye.

All week I had the strongest sensation my grandmother was no longer there.

There was no emotional attachment to the shape almost completely hidden beneath the shroud of sheets and blankets.

Suddenly, sometime during the early evening, I remember this because the news had just finished, I was aware of a change in the room. Everything was quiet. We were too emotionally exhausted for conversation, so when the sound came, although it was barely audible, we heard.

It was a voice, soft and hoarse from lack of use, but one I recognised because I had known it my entire life. It was my grandmother, and she was calling my name.

My mother and I both looked around, and as we turned our eyes met mirroring our astonishment. We could already see, from the corner of our vision that she was looking at us. Really looking at us. Her eyes were moving from one to the other, and there was no doubt about it, she knew exactly who we were.

All at once, in a split second, time reversed and the status quo was restored.

My grandmother was once more the matriarch of our small family: our rock.

We were speechless as she took one of our hands in each of hers and, just as she had so many times in the past, quietly told us everything would be all right. She explained she still loved us dearly, but she must go. More than that, she wanted to go.

She was not alone, she was with someone who had waited a long time for her, just, as she now assured us, she would wait for us.

I remember we returned the love she gave us. It was, as always, unconditional: she asked nothing in return. My grandmother was a wise woman. She never required promises which, when broken, would cause feelings of guilt and self reproach. My mother and I gave her a kiss on our nearest cheek and she was gone.

Oh not dead, although she might as well be: she was no longer there, and I guessed she would not be back. She had wandered off again, into a better place where I hoped her grandmother and George kept her company.

Why did she not die at that perfect moment? Because real life is not perfect; like some romantic book or film? Or, as I was later to learn, one more affair needed putting in order...

BETSY

This is the last week of my life – this life. When you leave for any journey there's a lot to do, and it's been hectic. So much to do, so little time. Loose ends to tie up, mainly at the hospital.

My doctor, without knowing it, has aided and abetted me in this, by prescribing powerful sedatives. As my spirit has grown stronger, my physical body has become weak, confused, and restless. With my brain medicated into forgetfulness I have been free to leave it to the care of nurses.

But tonight is different – I have business at home. So many goodbyes. This will be my last night on this earth, and, at the same time, the most painful and wonderful one.

How do I know this? Because I have had two visitors – oh not my well meaning, but often annoying, friends who have been visiting my breathing corpse. No, two very special people have come back for me. The first was my own dearest grandmother: she arrived a week ago and has been returning on and off ever since. Teaching me about this new world as she taught me about the last.

But tonight she was not alone, and I knew it was almost time to leave. Time is a strange thing: almost thirty years ago I became a widow, yet, as I meet George again, its like yesterday. I have one last duty, and must do it alone. Why I cannot say, but, like so many things now, I just know. Perhaps because at the moment I straddle two worlds which are divided. I fear that until people can open their minds and see the truth the gap will remain. As long as humanity is taught to fear or ridicule what it does not understand its chains will continue unbroken.

It is too big a question for me to answer, so I leave it, and my dearest George, to return home.

I think Beth is beginning to understand. Over the last few days there have been moments when I have been close to her, and she seemed to sense my presence. First of all I thought this was simply wishful thinking, but it is more than this. She appears to be able to read my thoughts. Yesterday I stood behind her as she gazed out into the blossoming garden. The thought suddenly crossed my mind how overgrown the lawn looked, when Beth turned, went outside and got out the mower.

Oh, of course, you cynics will claim coincidence, or a case of great minds thinking alike. I might agree with you, except when Beth turned she stepped around the empty space occupied by my spirit and whispered, "Yes I know."

Despite this growing conviction, I felt it better to speak to my daughters through more recognisable means. Margaret has always been fascinated by the supernatural, but never without a certain protective mockery. She is still too attached to the pleasures of this material world to accept mine.

So I made one final effort to reclaim my body. It was much easier than I thought.

There was little left in the diseased brain to resist me, and what remained was subdued by drugs. For a few precious minutes I took back control and said my goodbyes. It was good to see my girls together, although I was not so deluded to believe there would be any tearful reconciliation. It was enough for them to know I loved them, and for me to hear they loved me.

Once more I exit my body: the final departure. Yet I cannot leave this earth. I cannot die. Is this what ghosts experience – how long will I be trapped ? I linger on through the night: watching Beth go to her bed, and Margaret take up the night watch. And two questions keep running in circles around my mind.

Why am I still here? What is there left undone?

Just before the sun rises to brighten another day, at that darkest hour, I wonder if I will see it set. Then suddenly, the dawn arrives, chasing away the uncertainties of the night – and with it the jumble of my thoughts.

Everything becomes clear. I know what I am waiting for, and Beth is the only one who can give it to me…

Chapter Fifteen

An End and Beginning

ELIZABETH

I awoke on Sunday to a beautiful spring morning, and my mother gently shaking me into consciousness. At first I thought it was the worst, or best, news concerning Gran, but she quickly told me "no, it's all right, but the district nurse wants to see you." I was beyond appearances, so I dragged on yesterday's clothes and went downstairs where Mo was waiting. As I passed Gran's room I glanced in and saw mum sitting back down by the bed.

As I entered the living room the district nurse was finishing a cup of tea and wore the grave expression medics usually reserve for such awkward situations. But Mo was a kind-hearted soul, who had refused to become hardened by her daily exposure to misery. Over the last week we had developed a genuine relationship and her concern for us was not just professional, it was personal.

So when she told me Gran was near her end, she knew my feelings would be mixed. Yes there was the grief of loss, but also a guilty relief. She understood my dilemma and, over the last days, had tried to explain this was completely natural. But guilt, like resentment, is instinctive and not easily dismissed.

Self forgiveness may come over time, but at the moment there were more urgent issues.

Mo passed on the information I needed to accept now. In all likelihood my grandmother would not live to see another day. Her breathing was shallow and infrequent: all the signs of approaching death.

Mo promised to return later in the afternoon, but prepared me for the reality that my grandmother would probably no longer need her help.

She did leave one more piece of advice. All her experience had taught her what training had not. Apparently all nurses soon learn a valuable lesson when dealing with comatose and dying patients: keep talking.

Gran may be incapable of seeing me, but she could hear. If I had any unsaid words, now was the last chance to say them.

I thanked Mo and saw her to the door, then went upstairs to begin my watch.

Mum and I talked briefly about the situation, before she left for her own bed.

I looked down at Gran – her eyes were slightly open but did not move or even blink. I could barely hear her breathe, sometimes she paused and I held my own breath. Again that emotional tug of war: waiting for her next breath, while willing her not to take it.

We sat together, with the curtains pulled back letting in the sunlight, and the sash window slightly open to provide fresh air. There was only a slight breeze, just enough to move the lace curtains, but it carried with it all the hopeful aromas of early spring.

At some time during the morning I turned the Al Jolson tape off and the television on. There was a church service beginning which somehow seemed suitable, even though the seasonal sermon was about life rather than death. But then the minister went on to compare spring to rebirth, so perhaps it was apt after all! I hoped so.

We sat through it, like old times, joining in the well know hymns, except this time it was a solo performance. And if anyone heard my singing before, they would confirm this was not an uplifting experience!

All the while I held Gran's hand. It was almost lifeless, except for the very faint movement of a feeble pulse.

The programme ended and the announcer proclaimed the start of the London marathon. I remember thinking they would have perfect conditions: dry but cool.

In fact most of these thoughts had been spoken aloud. Talking to Gran as though she could hear my voice. It didn't seem at all strange: we had always shared our feelings in the past. Today was no different, it was just a little more special. Too special to waste on mundane chatter.

So as the army of fun runners began to slowly walk past the start posts, I continued to grasp her hand and talk. But this time the conversation was different. While I talked I stroked her forehead and told her it would be OK. I promised to look after everything, and this time it was a promise I was happy to make. I knew it would be kept.

Then all at once I felt an old regret resurface, and, for the umpteenth time during these final days, asked my grandmother to forgive me. For what?

Thoughts from the dark side of your brain which can never be forgotten. Words once spoken, which can never be erased.

There had been many moments over the last ten years when exhaustion and frustration had made me less than caring. If I was rational I would recognise we are all human and to expect perfection is setting yourself up for failure. But I was too emotional for reason and could only excuse myself with the consolation that I had been angry with the situation, never with her.

I never stopped loving my Grandmother: too much to want her to stay in this awful cruel existence.

Suddenly with this selfless thought, came out the words: "and I forgive you for anything you think you may have done to me." Not very poetic, or even grammatical, but from the heart, or some other part of my being. I don't know where – but like my grandmother I have a gift. This emerges when I am not thinking rationally – and is strongest when I am not thinking at all. When I act on pure instinct.The thought spoken, I kissed her on the cheek, as we had done every night of our lives. As I did so I heard a small sigh.

After days and nights of futile dread and hope I hadn't really expected anything to happen. And this time nothing did. As the seconds passed, while I held my own breath, all was silence.

I pulled back, and just stared down at my grandmother's face. All the age lines, won over years of hard work, had gone. The skin was flawless, but somehow unnatural, and I had a strange sense of déjà vu . Many years ago, as a child, I had been taken to Madame Tussaud's. There I stood over a model of the "sleeping beauty" and gazed in wonder as primitive electronics caused her chest to rise and fall.

This is how my grandmother now looked: a waxwork, but with the only movement a tiny pulse in her neck. As I watched even this stopped like the mechanism of a worn out clock.

She was gone, yet somehow she felt closer to me than ever before.

BETSY

Once the light had literally dawned on me, I went back to the hospital. I now knew why I was still here, and time was very very short. I visited the morgue, where my body would never lie, to say my goodbyes. At this time of the morning I knew most of my current waiters would be there, and psychic ties would pull the rest. Many of them, I was selfishly pleased to learn, were sad to see me go. Just a couple had difficulty hiding their envy, but such is human nature. I could not blame them: I have been guilty of the same offence.

With the last farewell wished, I left and headed to my corridor for the last time.

Although it was hardly mine any more. I would not need it. I had my own guides.

But I did have an appointment there: I had a final farewell to make – well actually two.

As I turned into the familiar corridor I saw three figures ahead of me. One was walking into the light while two turned and walked back towards me. As they drew close I found myself overwhelmed by hugs and licks. I had picked my successors well. Emma and Bob. It was their corridor now.

They had exercised their power of free will, in the best possible way, and chosen not to follow Vicky into the light.

Although they were my choice, the decision

was all theirs, and they were a perfect match. It was moving to leave them both, but it was not grief. I knew I would see them again, and in the meanwhile the hospital was in safe hands – and paws!

Everything done at the hospital, and a quick detour to visit Jenny and Susan at the nursing home, I headed back home, but not alone. If I had to wait then I would have the best company: my husband.

But somehow I had the feeling it would not be long. Beth and I had a special bond, so perhaps cutting the lawn was not the only appeal I could make to her!

We spent a wonderful morning, the three of us, like old times: listening to the church service. OK it was Church of England, but you can't have everything!

Afterwards I watch sadly as Beth asks again for my forgiveness – there was never any need.

Then unbelievably, all my prayers are answered. My grand daughter holds me close whispering the precious words I have waited for, and I accept her forgiveness so gratefully like the blessed miracle it is.

The sense of release is incredible and indescribable to you mere mortals.

But even through this startling sensation, another came to me. Although as light as a feather it took my breath away – my last breath. Beth, my beloved grand daughter, had gently kissed my cheek – we had said our last goodnight. I feel George's hand on my shoulder and know it is time to go.

So my dearest child I am ready to take that last giant step. Until we meet again God bless you my sweetheart, and make the most of the rest of your life.

Do not waste precious time in grieving for me, I am not there.